MW00328263

I devoured these spiky, knowing, unforgettable stories, which keenly dissect the dangers of girlhood, of womanhood, in America. Jenny Irish writes with vast insight, surprising jolts of humor, and true empathy for her characters and the broken world that made them.
—**Belle Boggs, author of** *The Gulf* **and** *The Art of Waiting*

In this collection of stories, Jenny Irish's sparse, raw prose gathers briny New England interiors, the eyes of old dogs, absent mothers and cold lovers. Each character is filled with the ache of absence, each story a Russian doll packed with glass. You'll want to cradle them to your chest, even knowing that, as you open them, the shards will cut you. A quiet, confident, and unassuming work.
—**Jen Michalski, author of** *The Summer She Was Under Water*

Often slyly funny and always devastatingly observant, Jenny Irish writes about the precarities of our moment with gorgeous prose and heartbreaking acuity.
—**Laura Kipnis, author of** *Unwanted Advances*

In *I Am Faithful*, Jenny Irish dissects the American corpus with a surgeon's precision, exposing the both the beauty and ugliness beneath the quotidian surface. These are powerful and unsettling stories, and their publication establishes Irish as a truth-teller of the highest order: lyrical, insightful, and admirably fearless.
—**Adam Wilson, author of** *What's Important Is Feeling*

Lovely, brutal, and absolutely mesmerizing. Jenny Irish is a genius, and *I Am Faithful* is a revelation.
—**Jennifer duBois, author of** *The Spectators*

In her wonderful debut collection of stories, Jenny Irish brings us up close to a darkly personal cast of women as they struggle through pain, loss, and transformation. Irish fixes her gaze on the difficult terrain where beauty and meaning are often found among the wreckage. By focusing on the sites of their wounds, we are asked to consider all that her characters have lost and overcome as we are invited to change alongside them. In a world that seems to require at times our loss of hope, *I Am Faithful* is an intimate proclamation of faith.
—**Jarret Middleton, author of** *Darkansas*

Jenny Irish's stories are unflinching glimpses into messy human lives. Finely crafted, the beautiful sentences build. There is ache, there is longing, and then, inevitably, the story bares its teeth.
—**Callan Wink, author of** *Dog Run Moon*

The characters in *I Am Faithful* live in the ever-more-uncertain American margins, riding the line between transgression and transcendence, searching for something worthy of the terrifying gift of their faith. In sentences exactingly detailed, blackly comic, and genuinely poignant, Jenny Irish writes prose for the body: her stories stick to your ribs, jostle your heart, jag your muscles with their rhythm and thwack. *I Am Faithful* is a wondrous book.
—**Murray Farish, author of *Inappropriate Behavior***

There's poetry woven through these stories, a word not wasted, making Irish's characters luminous and present. A person's past is never a thing left behind but the battered motor dragging them ever forward. Jenny Irish writes without fear, divulging the truths that we humans so often keep from one another. Each story resonates through its final sentence.
—**Bojan Louis, author of *Currents***

I AM FAITHFUL

Jenny Irish

Black
Lawrence
Press

Black
Lawrence
Press

www.blacklawrence.com

Executive Editor: Diane Goettel
Cover Design: Zoe Norvell
Book Design: Amy Freels
Cover Art: "Am" by Deborah Williams

Copyright © Jenny Irish 2019
ISBN: 978-1-62557-011-6

All rights reserved. Except for brief quotations in critical articles or reviews, no part of this book may be reproduced in any manner without prior written permission from the publisher: editors@blacklawrencepress.com

Published 2019 by Black Lawrence Press.
Printed in the United States.

For Mike

Contents

I am Faithful

For a week now in the apartment below mine there's been a tiny baby, brand new to the world. When it cries what comes through the floorboards are the sounds of a catfight. Nothing human, not even close, but still the noise registers as *child in need* and pulls me from sleep by the hair. Then, lacking a baby of my own, under the direction of some biological force set askew, I check on my dog.

She's small and sturdy-looking, black and white, and sleeps as if in mid-leap, front paws tucked high against her chest, rear paws level with the line of her spine, toes pointing back. I look at her and think of nursery rhymes. *And the cow jumped over the moon...*

The inability to ignore a baby's cry is not exclusive to humans, or even mammals. It affects almost every living thing. I learned this from PBS, watching a documentary where the narrator paused meaningfully after instructing viewers to contemplate a reptile's capacity for love.

Crocodiles were the example on screen. Hatchlings chirp when threatened, and in response mother-crocodile—no matter what she's doing, even in the second spin of a death roll, ripping loose a limb to swallow—drops everything, rushing to her young. She opens her mouth—jaws that can cleave a snorkeling Floridian into torso and trunk—and the hatchlings, so small rattlesnakes will swallow them whole, dart inside to be cradled in their mother's teeth.

I tell my boss, "It's supposed to be that bad." She's just become a grandmother for the fourth time over, but when she last watched the kids, bagged-out after an hour. When the baby wouldn't stop crying, she started to.

I consider, but decide against telling her about the young couple in Florida who slept while their dog chewed seven toes off the wrinkled pink feet of their infant son. The father was out back in a hammock, the mother napping just up the hall. Their lawyer has insisted neither parent heard a thing: exhaustion. But it was a neighbor on the other side of a vacant lot who called the police with a noise complaint.

Dispatch took a recording. "The people up the street," the neighbor says, "have a weasel in a trap." She takes a drag off a cigarette, and apologizes, "Sorry," a faint tremor in her voice. "My nerves are shot." In the background a dishwasher is running, and under the churn of water and rattle of cutlery, there's a high, desperate yowling. "Can you hear it?" she asks. "That's been my day. Can someone get out here and put the thing out of its misery?"

Lately, my feeling about Florida is: Let's call in Bugs Bunny with the saw. But then I think of the Everglades and am forced to re-evaluate.

"It's okay," I tell my boss. "Everyone's in one piece."

"Still kicking," she agrees.

"And screaming."

She shakes her head, "You're a smartass." But isn't upset, because almost immediately, she does her standard line: "I wish I wasn't out of sons."

She believes I have a sense of humor, a decent figure, and good mothering potential. My getting married has become a great concern of hers. "You can't blame me," she says. "I'm a product of my culture."

What she is, is a member of The Junior League, a native Texan, broad-shouldered, sun-tanned, and blonde, a once-upon-a-time oil heiress from the old society days when it was better to have a husband who beat you bloody than be single. Because of this, her perfect front teeth are false and one eye opens wider than the other. For lack of marriageable sons, she swears she'll find me a man who's good to his dogs. According to her, this is the surest way to gauge quality in the opposite sex.

At night, I sometimes wonder, what would it be like to share a bed? Bodies naturally fit to one another. There is evidence, in caves, in France, that our human ancestors spent the dark and terrifying nights tumbled together in piles like puppies. Starting sleep, I assume a starfish pose, all my limbs tossed wide to fill the empty space. Waking, I am always tucked tightly to myself. But, I've seen too many heartbreak articles: mothers crawling into the blankets with their babies at their breasts, who then roll in the night, to invite my dog to join me. She is not so small as a newborn, but neither, I have been told, is she so sturdy as she looks.

Rather than bring her to my bed, I go to hers. Hand cupped a millimeter from her damp black nose, her breathing is steady and soft against my palm. Inhale, exhale—as it should be. A band of eye-white shows between furred lids. A paw twitches. She is dreaming. Gently, I drag a finger along her spine, touching the way I've watched the veterinarian do, feeling her vertebrae lined up neatly.

"Something here," the veterinarian had said, fingers pressing to my dog's back. "Just here." She took my hand to guiding it. "Feel?"

"No," I said.

The veterinarian's hand was a weight on mine, "Feel?"

"I don't feel anything."

"Well," she said, "it's there."

In fourteenth-century wedding portraits, the bride is traditionally dressed in green—a call-back to our pagan pasts—with a dog at her feet. I learned this on a museum tour from a docent who consulted note cards poorly hidden in his jacket sleeve. It was unlikely, he explained, that the dogs found in these paintings had any relationship to the couples posing. In fact, it was unlikely there was a dog in the room at any time.

At the end of the tour, this was the one question that I asked: So if it's not their dog, why is it there? Because, the docent said, _Fido_, the most popular of dog names, is Latin for _I am faithful_.

It takes a short series of intuitive leaps to understand that explanation. Here's a joke that works the same way: Why do women have legs? So they don't leave a trail. Or another: What's the difference between pink and purple? The grip. Here's a joke that I prefer: What did the dyslexic, agnostic, insomniac do? Stayed up all night, worrying about the meaning of Dog.

My father's idea of humor was to spread his hands and say, "It's a dog's life." By which he meant that dogs are the family members we can murder without the threat of serious consequence. To my mother, laughing, he would say, "You're so miserable, if you were a dog, I'd take you out back and shoot you."

In that spirit, this is, for me, *The Waste Land* of jokes: A man and a boy are walking in the woods. It's getting dark. The boy says, "I'm scared!" And the man replies, "I don't know what *you're* complaining about! *I'm* the one that's gotta walk outta here alone!"

My first boyfriend never had a dog. A family like that: mother, father, and son—by the time I came along, they should have been on their second or third Golden Retriever, or big blond Labrador, or have had a Boxer for a guard dog, at least. The kids I went to school with, the children of his social class, had fathers who showed a preference for Boxers. Growing up, I knew a mess of Beaus, Rockys, and Brutuses. They slept on plaid flannel beds by stonework fireplaces, doing an odd double-duty, family pet and intended menace.

As I hung my sweater on the child-high hooks those houses always had, the father would come down the hall, crouching to ask, "Are you scared of dogs?" I wasn't. "It's a big dog," the father would caution. Then, when the animal came flying into the room, he would make a show of holding it back. "It's okay. It's okay," he would say, as the dog, over-eager, lunged against his grip.

At birthday parties there were little girls who would twist and scream, though their own dogs at home behaved the same way. Sixty pounds of unchecked enthusiasm, the worst they would do was knock someone over, step on them a little, slobber on their face. But still, girls would cry themselves sick. Some had to go home.

The mother in the house would hiss, "Could you do something with that animal!" until the father gave up giving un-obeyed commands, and finally, bribed the dog away. Leading it, not outside to a chain strung from tree to woodshed, or soldered to a metal spike hammered into the ground. Lured clear of the company, the dogs were "put up"—a phrase I've heard instructing children who are done with their toys, but leave them strewn about—in a plastic kennel, or wicker cage raised on wooden feet, kept in a clean corner, at the back of the kitchen, or in the foyer, or in the cool darkness of some spare unused space upstairs.

My father kept dogs, and was particular about them in the way that other men are the cars they'll drive, or the women they'll date. Within a month of my mother leaving him, he had a new woman moved in. She was a dishrag soul, and he treated her as a dog, absent the respect he gave chosen members of that species. He refused to be seen with her in public, but liked having her around the house. Without expectations for her treatment, she seemed grateful to be of service and was content to be reprimanded—warranted or not—so long as it meant she might eventually be forgiven.

But, about the things that truly mattered to him, my father had his standards. Red Nose Pit Bulls were his dog of choice: forty pounds of muscle and snap. His were smaller than generally preferred in sporting-circuits, but were all descendants of a lion-eyed Irish Old Family Dog named Haul, a celebrity so far as an animal who has never taken or saved a human life can be, a weight-pull champion on dirt, snow, and rails. It was a pedigree that forgave my father's dogs their size.

Before the pit bulls, there was a high-strung Doberman, and later, an inherited Rottweiler bitch, and overlapping, an assortment of small, long-lived lapdogs with free run of the house: my mother's pets. With their little faces between her hands, she would say, "I sha'n't be gone long—you come too." So we all knew some Robert Frost by heart—me, and the dogs alike.

Once, I found my college roommates, three Connecticut blondes, gathered around a newspaper, making shrill noises of excitement and distress. I assumed their enthusiasm to be over horoscopes, an especially favorable alignment of the stars. "Wait until you hear this," one said. "It's the worst thing ever." Then I thought there must have been a rape or robbery or killing on campus, and because of it, the cancellation of some event—no midnight swimming, or XXX bingo in the Union.

But no—

They were beside themselves over a man with more puppies than he could find homes. He shot two without any problem, but the third wouldn't stop squirming, making it difficult to aim. When he went down on his knees to pin it, there was an accident positioning the barrel. The puppy somehow managed to shoot the man, and he eventually died from the wound. The *worst thing*, the thing that so moved my roommates, was not the man's death, but his intention.

There is, I think, an assumption of malice when we hear a story like that. But, what if it were only matter-of-fact? Like, there's a kind of man who shoots a dog, because a dog is a dog. He's the same man who drowns newborn puppies by the sack-full every spring then ticks it from the list of chores in his head. He's seen the public service announcements: *Spay and neuter your pets*. But, he doesn't have pets. He has dogs. He's the same kind of man who is superstitious of bodies opened and altered. He doesn't say so—he wouldn't say so—but he believes the medical-arts to be a sort of dark magic. Doctors make him sweat. He's a man who doesn't admit to fear, and so when he is afraid he is angry. He's the man who dies of a slowly consuming cancer, an abscess left to fester. He's the man taken down by a clogged valve in his heart, thirty slow years in the making. That kind of man: he's a tough old bastard, but he's never meant any harm. On the anniversary of his death, his sons drink, because their father was a tough old bastard and they hated him, but he never meant any harm, and they loved him too.

The Rottweiler—I do not call it *our*—came to us through an act of would-be kindness. Someone died who had loved it very much. Rather than have the dog put down, it was given to our family, who didn't want it, but couldn't refuse it, and it lived outside on a wire run. In the coldest weather, my father brought it into the house, but kept it chained on a short length screwed to the mudroom floor. Not cruelty—it was a dog. There was a blanket for it between the drying wood and winter boots. But the Rottweiler was not allowed into the house proper, and so it was kept chained, because before, brought inside, it would not stay where it was told, was always belly-sliding forward, the tips of claws-then-feet-then-muzzle creeping into carpeted rooms where it neither belonged nor was welcome to be.

I love my dog in a way that defies description and qualifiers, though those are all I have to offer. *She's my dog.* I love the way her feet smell: like corn chips or warm bread or waffles, depending on the day. I love her wet nose on my neck, the two of us on the couch, her laid out on my chest like a baby. I love how she freezes when she sees a dove then drops to her belly and stalks it, the tips of her ears showing above the overgrown grass. I love her flat, comedienne face. I love her sense of humor. She has one—I know it. I love her bulbous, salty eyes that I sometimes kiss by mistake when we are playing our silliest game: Torture of a Thousand Kisses. I love how she is cold after being reprimanded, how she sulks, how as revenge she will steal small electronics and hide them—my misplaced phone found buried under a pillow. I love her mind.

Here is a true story: when she was just a puppy, I signed my dog up for obedience classes. The training method involved a small metal "clicker" and treats given as reward for commands obeyed. "Sit," I said, clicking, and when she sat, I clicked again, and fed her a little biscuit. The evening after that first class, I heard the sound of the clicker—*click-klok-click-klok*—coming from the kitchen, and there was my dog, sitting at attention, working it with her mouth, looking up at the jar of Milk Bones on the countertop. And if that doesn't prove her intelligence, there's this: she knows how to dance. We do The Madison together to oldies rock. I do not hold her in my arms. I step, this way, that way, forward and back, and she, my little monkey, mirrors me.

My dog, a particularly blunt veterinarian told me, is "compromised." Meaning, she has a series of health issues, which will, as she ages, create more. Asked for her honest opinion, the veterinarian pulled no punches. "She'll have no quality of life," she said then offered a solution I rejected. The vet walked us to the door, where she knelt and took my dog's head in her hands. "It's your job," she said, looking up at me, tilting my dog's face toward mine, "to take care of her. She depends on you."

My father spent most of his time with his pit bulls, walking the property line, visiting each one, touching their short-cropped ears and rubbing balm into the cracked pads of their feet. Sometimes he took them all off their runs, brought them up onto the lawn and arranged them in a row. When he held his hand flat they dropped and turned to stone, a line of sphinxes waiting for the next command.

My dog is a little terrier, genetically fitted with giant conical ears that are as expressive as her eyes. Cropping and docking have only recently passed out of fashion for her breed. Even five years ago she'd have been done up like a Doberman—ears cut into high, tapering points, her tail docked at the cartilage, like a thumb taken off at the knuckle.

Historically, dogs' ears were cropped not for aesthetics, but for safety and ease of upkeep, the same theory that has been applied, for centuries, to the shaving of the heads of soldiers. Ratters and fighting dogs, sport baiters paired against bulls and bears and wolverines, as well as their own brothers and sisters in the ring, and, in more domestic settings, the quick little terriers on guard against various barnyard varmints—for them, dangling ears made a tender grip for the enemy. Removing the pinna, the outer flesh, kept the thin, unprotected skin, from being caught between teeth and shredded into fringe.

There are still sand-floored rings made with scraped up plywood and two-by-four supports. Ears cut tight to the skull and angled back—a battle crop—is emblematic of a fighting dog. But what's a benefit in a fight becomes a hindrance outside of it. Exposed, into the fragile labyrinth of the inner ear goes rainwater, goes dirt, goes insects. Dogs are left deaf from the complications of a bad crop. Their whole head becomes an infection. Not so irregularly, they die from it.

Docking is what's done to the tail, and is a lesser procedure. The Romans believed it could prevent rabies. On a working dog, the absence of a tail is a few less inches to pick up burrs. My father, who quizzed me on trivia that interested him, did his docking and dewclaws both with a pocketknife at the kitchen table when the puppies were three days old. Cropping, if a person has any sort of discretion, should wait until the dog is older, when how to shape the ears to best flatter the skull can be reasonably judged. Most of my father's dogs lived. Few scarred. I have read that bears lick their babies into shape.

After my boyfriend—the one who'd never had a dog—left for college, his parents bought a puppy. An ash gold Lhasa Apso: The Tibetan lion-dog. She patrolled the house, warning off the mailman with a surprisingly aggressive bark. As she grew, she would gnash her teeth at the open mail slot. They took her to a trainer, and were disappointed to learn that their dog's forefathers were carefully bred to serve as guards. The behaviors they did not like were living in her blood. She might be trained against them, but could not be un-taught instinct.

In their antiquity, Lhasa Apsos followed intruders from room to room, barking an alert to the Temple monks. "I didn't want an aggressive animal," my boyfriend's mother said, and after an anxious year, had the dog put down.

Our Doberman was partially skinned, dragged through a quarter-open car-door-window one sunny August morning by a square-jawed Mastiff, who had clambered over the pickets of a fence three houses up the street from the post office. My mother was inside doing errands, and I was a small child left dozing in the car with the Doberman on watch. The mastiff, a dog more substantial in both size and violence, caught our Doberman by his skinny throat, teeth punching through the double folds running the length of his neck, and by that slippery grip—tearing through thin, wadded flesh, and snapping, biting deeper—was trying to pull our Doberman through the window gap, out to meet his death. The Mastiff was succeeding. One ear peeled cleanly back from our Doberman's picky skull. It hung there, dangling at his neck like a black balloon leaked of all its air, and I slept. At first, I was sleeping—a small child blowing bubbles of spit, strapped into a booster seat, left safe, though the car doors did not lock, protected by our Doberman.

I can remember my mother saying, "I'll be right back. Two shakes of a lamb-y-kins tail," then drowsing in the heat.

My mother, just through the post office's double doors, was using the pink sponge on the counter to moisten strips of glue tape, sealing boxes of old books to ship off to Florida in exchange for oranges—a system of trade I still don't understand. When the oranges came, some would be rotten, pulsing with bugs, but others were perfect, shining, and the fruit inside was the warm lick-able color of the tiles in the changing room at the pool. In secret I sometimes licked those tiles, expecting sharp flavor. I can remember the oranges, and the orange of the tiles—their smoothness against the slight, pebbled roughness of my tongue—and in the grocery, when I pass the pyramids of citrus fruits, I smell chlorine, and sometimes, with scars to show, I tell the story of how our Doberman saved my little life. But what he really did was shit on me in his panic, and with his flailing hind feet—not the Mastiff's teeth at all—tear my skin open, deep, almost to the bone.

I jerk awake to an animal squall. My heartbeat is in my throat, dizzying. Before I've thought to do it, the covers are flicked back. I'm moving down the hall. Against my soles the floorboards quiver faintly, possessed by the baby's cries. Now that I recognize the sound—the infant below in a fit—I could turn back to bed, spread out, let my pulse slow, and invite sleep come again, but instead, I check on my dog.

She is asleep, unbothered by the baby's bawling, stretched long, front legs extended, stiff, one hind leg back, the other tucked to her belly. I take it by the foot, pulling gently, straightening. I will line it up with the other limb. As her knee bends there is a *crack*, not so pure a sound as a tree branch snapped, but still sharp, and my dog, instantly awake, flinches from my touch.

My father put our Doberman down himself. He wrapped the dog in a tarp to keep the blood off his clothes, then carried it to the edge of the woods and shot it in the head. It was in bad shape, suffering. What he did was probably the kinder thing. When my boyfriend's parents put their Lhasa down, the veterinarian gassed it into pliancy first, so they could hold it like a baby—have a calm farewell. After they were satisfied, an injection was administered.

As a child I had perfected sneaking out my window and made a regular practice of it in the quiet pre-dawn hours of early morning. The pit bulls would stand silent. They did not cock their heads like others dogs, but looked straight-on. In the semi-dark their eyes were gold. They were gentle and dignified, grandfatherly in their affection. A wet nose against my knee in greeting, a soft exhale. They were not much for licking—the occasional touch of a warm tongue against an extended hand. Calm, they would resettle into the cool furrows they'd dug into the dirt, and I would lie down with them.

From the outside, I would see the house light one window at a time, a trail from my parents' bedroom, through the kitchen, leading down the hall to the bathroom. I waited—pressed belly-low on the damp earth, chin hooked over a watchful dog's back—for the time that one of them, my mother or my father, would make the two extra steps from the bathroom to my bedroom door, and check on me in my bed, only to find me missing from it. Snails made slow progress across my bare arms, and I thought how it would be to have to reveal myself to them, slinking up from the fields to the door like the dog gone through the gate called home again. But they never made the few steps—those two steps—more.

Five A.M., thereabouts, and the stars were flour handprints. My father's truck rumbled in the driveway while he smoked a cigarette, leaning against its waxed bright door. Inside the house, my mother, followed by her little dog, moved from room to room, her head distorted by curlers. They were, in their own way, people who looked after things.

The beneficiary of another man's soured luck, my father bought a fishing camp for a song. He began to spend his weekends on the clear blue water, alone in an aluminum boat, luring trout from the cold shadows of submerged boulders. His time otherwise committed, he lined the pit bulls up on the back lawn and sold them at a makeshift auction. In the swagger of certain men, I saw that the dogs would not live well when they left us. My father had cared for them, because they were *his*, and these men would hurt them, because they were *theirs*.

When it was over, my father's pockets fat with folds of bills, and all the dogs hoisted into the beds of trucks and tied down like lengths of timbers, I cried. They were already gone, but I cried as if tears could save them. When I wouldn't stop, my father took me by the shoulders. He said it wouldn't be fair, anymore, to keep them. I said it was not fair to *me*, not to. He walked me back until my back was against the kennel wall. He said to me, "You're crying over *dogs*."

The other day, I was talking to a man, a work acquaintance, someone I like, but don't know well enough for conversation between us to be easy, and so we were talking about our dogs. If we had children, we would have traded stories about them. In their absence, we wowed one another with the accomplishments of our canis familiaris. He had a goofball mix, Dachshund and Shepherd. We did the old joke: *How'd that happen? I'm not completely sure, but a ladder was involved.* We were laughing over it, blushing, and between us there was a sudden a little bubble of warmth.

"See?" My boss said. "See?" She moved behind me and began to arrange my hair in a pile on top of my head. "You can't see this," she said, "but this is an updo that would look great on a date."

"I'm not interested."

She let my hair fall, coming around to stand in front of me, hands on her hips. After a moment, she spun herself across the floor, "Dinner! Dancing!" Recovering from a one-person-dip, wrapped in her own arms, she moaned, "Love."

"Disappointment," I said. "Inevitable heartbreak."

She threw her hands up.

Later, she reappeared, and though hours had passed, continued, "And he's funny too." In her hand was an invisible checklist that she marked with flourish.

Beyond goodness to dogs, her lesser criteria included, *no one like your father*—by which she meant her own—and *actually funny*. According to my boss, her father's idea of humor was to walk into the room eating a garlic dill pickle when she was suffering with the stomach flu. "Boy-o-boy," he'd say, chewing, open mouthed, "this is one juicy sucker."

But if there is one kind of man, then isn't there also another? He claims he's the same kind of man as the first. He's the kind of man who shoots a dog, and says a dog is a dog, but really, he's just the kind of man who likes to shoot a dog. He likes how it walks beside him, obedient to its death. He's the same man who drowns puppies by the sack-full every spring and enjoys ticking it from the list of chores in his head. He's seen the public service announcements: *Spay and neuter your pets.* But, nobody tells him what to do with his goddamn dogs. He doesn't say so, he wouldn't say so, but he revels in the power of injury, both caused and received. He's always angry, never satisfied with the attention paid to him. He's the same man who feels a sickness in his body and curls around it. He's the man who screams the surgeon is a witch doctor and throws his tray at the nurse. His wife and sons apologize to him, and later, far from earshot, apologize for him. When he recovers, his sons drink, because their father is a tough old bastard, who all his life has set out to do harm and they hate him, and they love him too.

The baby, crying through the floor, wrenched me from a dream. In it, my dog and I were at a fair. We walked arm in arm, the way girlfriends who have known one another since childhood do. We had two tickets left, and toured the grounds slowly, trying to choose our final ride. Each breath was nauseating and delicious, the air dense with the hot smells of manure, fry oil, trampled grass, burnt sugar, and industrial grease. What we settled on was The Tunnel of Love, and boarded our flimsy plywood boat with laughter ready in our throats. Green double doors painted with vines and fronds opened into darkness—black water, black air. Then, like Christmas lights on a faulty length of wire, blinking two at time, on then off, returning with a half a dozen burning bulbs, then two dozen, a bright stutter becoming a steady glow, the water was marked with golden cuts of illumination. As we floated past, I saw the lights were eyes. Their flickering showed us a cave—stalactites, stalagmites—a cage of teeth, cradling us together.

I go, and I check on my dog. She's a sleeping crescent of soaring muscle and bone. *And the cow jumped over the moon . . .*

Her dreams must be full of flight. Clearing the top strand of barbed-wire that divides one grazing field from the next, or over the pickets of a low white fence that would keep her in a small, neat yard, domestic—or maybe she, an instinctual killer, hangs suspended with a dream rabbit's white neck a jaw-snap away, waiting, raw with longing, for her teeth.

An appointment made must be kept. This is basic etiquette. Normally, in the car, for safety's sake, I make my dog stay in the passenger seat. But today I let her have my lap, and I drive so slow that she can put her head out the window and draw big bully snorts of air without having to squint against the force of the wind.

In the parking lot, my heart is a gyroscope, its momentum failing. I clip on her leash. I would like to carry her, but she is shivering with excitement, pulling against the pace I would set. Smart girl: she knows what doors free biscuits live behind. We jog because she wants to. I stop at the stairs. She climbs them. I can't. I have to hold the railing. For a moment she's patient with delay then looks back at me and whines. Because my heart is red wreckage, and because she cannot know it, I joke with her. I say, "I don't know what *you're* complaining about."

I'm the one, after all, that'll be walking out alone.

Borning

The man, who for a time I thought of as a father, had wanted to sleep with me for the better part of a year before we did it. Initially, I misunderstood his interest, welcoming it as paternal. His flirtation, his habit of inviting me to meals, his insistent giving of gifts, I misread as fatherly affection.

He clarified.

Fuck was the word he used most often, though in some of his more purple correspondences he chose softer language, preferring then *make love, share absolutely, succumb to awe.*

As a younger man, he'd planned to be a poet.

Side-by-side at a restaurant where the meals were assembled from things I couldn't, with any confidence, pronounce, he watched me eat. "You're like a bird," he said, and was excited by the observation.

From the chalkboard behind the bar, I had ordered the special by pointing. It involved larded bread and endive and sausage crème. Uncertain what to expect, I hoped I would know how to eat it. Only in the last year had I learned why pasta was served with a large spoon, why the lemon at fancy seafood restaurants came not cut in wedges, but halved and tied in a square of cheesecloth.

On other chilled afternoons, in other dim, wood-paneled rooms, the man had been a kind teacher. He demonstrated how to twirl linguini into the tight spiral of a miniature wasp's nest, and under the flat silver eye of a striped silver fish rippling the length of its tank had touched my knee when I began to un-swaddle the lemon at edge of my plate, explaining, "The cloth acts as a filter to catch any pulp or seeds."

I was embarrassed, and he gave my leg a quick, hard squeeze. "No one knows anything before they learn it." He was smiling. "I like teaching you new things."

On delivery, the special revealed itself to be an oblong, single-serving pizza. Something I could eat with my hands.

I was not quite twenty. The man was more than old enough to be my father, and also he was my boss. He signaled the end of our meal by closing a hand around my wrist, turning it to show how his thumb and middle finger overlapped. "Look at that." I pulled lightly. He kept his hold. "There's nothing to you." He leaned in close, "You're just the littlest thing." I pulled again.

He let go, turning to gesture at a waitress hustling past with a loaded tray. A lash of spice trailed her. It had a heavy body-odor tang, like sweat cooled on bare skin then wrapped again in warm clothes—a smell like sex that I could taste in the back of my throat.

The man pushed away from the table with just-too-much force. His chair whined against the floor. Heads turned toward the sound.

"I'm sorry," I said.

"For what?" He took a fold of bills, held with a money clip, from his pocket.

"The waitress."

"The waitress?" He was looking past me out the tall windows. Two girls were slipping in slush on the sidewalk, grabbing at one another's elbows, laughing. "The service was fine." He cocked his head toward the girls. "They're enjoying themselves, at least."

I watched him arrange bills in a neat fan and pin them under his water glass. I asked, "Are you not having fun?"

"Are *you*?"

"What?"

"Having fun?"

"Am I having fun?"

He lifted my coat from the chair back and held it open so I could thread my arms through. Against my ear, he breathed, "Did you *enjoy* yourself?"

For a moment it was like I had forgotten all the words I'd ever known, and when I found them again what I said was "Thank you" instead of yes.

"Thank you?"

"Thank you."

He took me by the elbow, navigating us between tables, then stopped in the foyer, letting go of my arm to button his coat. "What are you thanking me for?"

"Lunch," I said. "Thank you for lunch."

The skin around his eyes pinched into folds. "Anything else? Anything else you want to thank me for?"

There were people all around, and his question felt louder than the hostesses, neat in black, asking softly, "Sir? Sirs?" and inviting, "This way, please," leading people back into the dim of the dining room. I could feel the eyes of the small groups of older men, administrators, or professors from the university, serious in wool and cashmere and leather gloves, appraising us as they waited. Trying to guess: father and daughter, or something else?

He prompted, "Anything else?"

"Everything," I said. "Thank you for everything."

He slotted the button at his throat, then took my arm, moving me toward the door, but was watching, still, the girls outside.

"Everything?" He was staring ahead, not looking at me. Both girls were in pleated plaid skirts, high, patterned socks, and riding boots, their bare slender hands and bare slender thighs mottled from the cold. "Anything in particular?"

I touched his hand resting on my sleeve. The skin was dry, starting to split, a pink crack opening deep over his knuckles. "This looks sore."

"Unsubtle." He said it like a reprimand. "You're trying to shift my attention. Answer the question."

In the middle of his life, he'd taught at a college, and the way he spoke to me, he had explained, was *Socratic*—question driven—because of it.

I could smell the cigarettes he'd smoked that morning, and under them the pine and lavender of his cologne, and under that, faintly, sweat, and a cool mineral dampness.

He walked me through the wide glass doors. Outside, the air was wet and gray. We stood arm in arm; I waited for him to take a step, to guide me. The girls were ahead of us on the sidewalk, continuing their slow progress. I couldn't think of what to say. I was wearing gloves he had given me—leather, lined with rabbit fur. A minute might have passed. Dirty melt-water was seeping into my shoes.

"Well?" He made a slow appraisal, looking me up and down, before releasing his hold on my arm. "Nothing else to say?"

I shook my head.

He flicked a hand at me, dismissing, "I've got other things to do."

I worked then at the library of the university where I was taking classes—the most famous of the famous ones in Massachusetts, which now trains its students to say they went to school in Boston, pause, and then correct themselves: *Well, Cambridge.* This approach, following a study that showed direct use of the university's name was intimidating to those without similar affiliation. Better to perform humility.

To be clear, I wasn't an attendee of any of the exclusive undergraduate colleges. Through a program that was a kissing-cousin to night school, I took the two-hundred-dollar classes open to anyone who had the two hundred dollars to pay. The instructors were not the university's famous professors, but young PhDs. Having found no better employment, they signed semester-by-semester contracts as underpaid adjuncts. In the heart of the day, they taught fundamentals to sub-standard freshman descended from families who had built America; at odd hours, they taught the same courses to the masses. I was working my way through.

This was the year my mother ran away. While my father was at work she packed her better things and left. I'd done the same after high school, but without secrecy. My new address was tacked in the cupboard above the hooks for keys. My cell phone number never changed.

For my father, my mother left a note. For me nothing, no warning, so I was lost when he called demanding, "Did you know? Did you know?"

Slowly, I pieced together what had happened, but couldn't think to pick my words. I asked, "Does it matter?"

"I knew it." He was pleased to think I had betrayed him.

At the library, my job was to find misplaced things. Though the Acquisitions Department had hired me, the purpose of my position was to *prevent* purchases. Every year, tens of thousands of dollars of library materials went missing, were replaced at significant cost, and later turned up again. I was supposed to find those things that were lost inside the building.

Books easily went astray. The person at the circulation desk might fail to check one in, or a student worker, sick of pushing a trolley through the stacks, would shove a volume wherever there was room on a shelf. It wasn't uncommon, either, for a borrower to accrue ridiculous overdue fees then sneak late books back into the library, leaving them somewhere strange and noticeable before coming to the circulation desk to make a small scene.

"I won't pay," they said. "I returned that book *years* ago."

I calmed them, filled out little cards of information, and went searching. Experience taught me not to start in the stacks. I found books on the turntables of the record players in the poetry room, and built into crude, miniature cabins on the center of the couch in the quiet study area, and on rainy days, with their pages damp, lined along the deep sill of the window in the landing of the back stairway.

I was responsible for calling the borrowers, apologizing for any inconvenience, and telling them all charges were reversed. I would thank them for their patience and their understanding and their continued patronage. Often, after that, they were kind. Occasionally, they thanked me in return. More frequently they volunteered, "I know none of this is *your* fault," then continued to list complaints, but in a milder tone.

Through work, apology was a skill I polished, and I could, after a half-year, with real sincerity, thank anyone for almost anything.

Since most of my time was spent trying to restore the mislaid to its proper place, I came to know the library like the house I'd grown up in—all its nooks and forgotten spaces. The great building kept no secrets from me.

I knew that on the third floor, in the solarium, the furniture was original, its arrangement unchanged since the building's opening. Each chair had worn tracks into the floor and on quiet afternoons would drift from tables as if haunted.

I knew, too, that the most graphic scenes in *The Story of O* were on pages dog-eared so often they'd lost their corners, and that page seven was missing from all three copies of the 1994 printing of *Tropic of Cancer*. I knew *Steal This Book* got stolen, but not as often as guides to divorce and self-helps about recovering from sexual abuse, and I knew that books shoved through the brass hatch of the after-hours drop slot could fall into the dark corner of the big collection bin and be lost for decades.

When my father called while I was at work—my cell phone buzzing like a wasp on the wrong side of the window glass—I knew all the unvisited places where I could answer without being caught.

Once, I slipped into an alcove full of bound issues of *The Saturday Evening Post*. Color copies of the covers were glued to the cardboard that held them. November 22, 1941 faced out, showing a girl with blonde curls held back with blue ribbons. She was saying a prayer over an empty plate while eyeing a roast turkey.

"Dad," I said. "I'm here."

"I've about had it." His voice was tight and low. "I'm about to paint this room red. I'm about to pull the trigger."

My father—who before my mother left would answer the phone with, "She's not here," and then hang up—was calling every day, promising to kill himself unless I told him where his wife was. *His wife*, who was also my mother, but he never acknowledged her tie to me.

"Don't say that."

"I'll say what I want."

"Please, Dad."

"Where is she?"

"I don't know."

"Where's my wife?"

"I don't know."

"I hope you can handle the guilt, 'cause I'm gonna blow my brains out."

"I don't know where she is."

"Bullshit."

Some days he called a dozen times.

My mother—she called once. In place of *Hello*, or, *Sweetheart*, she said, "I couldn't get reception before."

I could hear the drag of the wind and the rush of other cars. I thought it was strange: she was on the highway. Then I understood my father wasn't the only one who'd been left. I understood her *leaving* was literal, that she was going *away*. Though I hadn't ever before, I called her "Mommy."

"I'm saying goodbye," she said. "After this, you won't be able to reach me."

On a shelf in the oversized books section, *The Essential Calvin and Hobbes* was wedged between a copy of William Blake's illuminated works and an illustrated history of root vegetables. At the beginning of the semester, students who had enrolled in art surveys scuttled through the aisles like crabs, climbing, picking, and pinching from the shelves, but generally this was an area infrequently visited. I was looking for a missing copy of *Story of the Eye*, and I thought that if my father called, I could answer without concern for being caught slacking on the job—though I knew I wasn't the only one who took advantage of the emptiness.

Sometimes, I found cigarette butts tamped out on the armrests of the old vinyl chairs in the wide aisles. On one yellow seat there was a burn in the shape of an asterisk where hot ash must have fallen between open legs, an illustrated copy of *Fanny Hill* lying abandoned on the floor.

My phone buzzed against my hip. I answered, "Dad."

"You'll get ten thousand right away."

"What?"

"In the will." There was a pause. "Money. I bet that'd make you happy."

I fell into the burned chair and put my forehead against my knees. "You don't mean that."

"Don't I?"

"No."

"I don't?"

I closed my eyes, listening to him breathe.

"I'm hanging up on you," he threatened, then allowed a gap for me to speak, to stop him from disconnecting.

"Wait—" but he was already gone.

Unfolding, I saw a man standing at the end of the aisle. He was holding a hardcover book with a paper cup balanced on it, and a sandwich on a small paper plate balanced on top of that. He looked familiar—neat silver hair and a close-trimmed beard—but I couldn't place him.

"Boyfriend trouble?"

I had worried about being caught, about someone thinking poorly of me for taking personal calls at work, about the half-true explanations I would give, about written reprimands, about the job I needed put in jeopardy, but I had never thought about what I would sound like overheard.

A chill tickled down my spine, standing me up stiff and straight. When humiliation is described, it's always hot, hot, hot, but I've only ever felt it as cold. I tucked the phone away. "My father."

The man smiled, teeth perfectly shaped. "That's sweet," he said. "A daddy's girl."

Angling around him at the end of the aisle, I could smell cigarettes on his clothes.

"You can't eat up here. Or smoke." I gestured at the books, floor to ceiling.

Later, that same day, I saw the man again. He was coming up the narrow back stairs as I was going down. In an awkward hold—one arm twisted underneath—he was carrying a box of papers. I could tell the cardboard flaps on the bottom were loose. Backtracking to the landing, I cleared the way and, looking down, recognized him all at once: the librarian who was not only *my* boss, but everyone else's, too. I hadn't ever met him, but his photograph hung in the lobby above a plaque etched with his name.

When he reached the landing, he was winded. I stepped close to press a hand under the box, supporting the straining seam. "Let me help," I said.

Our fingers brushed. His were cool and dry as they moved against mine. Together, slowly, we made it up the final flight of stairs with the box intact, fingers wound together in a safety net under its bulging bottom.

"Good girl," he said.

I thanked him.

In the drugstore, I debated: what did I need more, tampons, or Midol? What was in my cabinet? Neither. Nothing. I had discovered the ATM wouldn't allow a withdrawal smaller than twenty dollars and there was less than that in my account.

My father was at the store, too, calling from the bread aisle of the market near the house where I grew up, needing to know what he would eat: "What kind of bread do I like?" I gave him the brand my mother had always bought, told him, from memory, exactly what was printed on the bag.

"This place is full of women," he said. "It's humiliating."

Further up the drugstore aisle a stock boy was loading adult diapers onto a shelf.

My father said, "I'm the only man here."

"Dad…"

"You could help."

"I want to." I picked up a pink plastic-wrapped box, then put it back. "Tell me how I can."

"You could tell me where my wife is."

"I don't know."

"Bullshit," he said.

"Let me buy you a drink," the man said.

"I'm not old enough."

He laughed. "A Shirley Temple, then? A tea?" Mock-solemn, a hand over his heart, he said, "I am indebted to you."

Outside, the air was brisk, touched with smoke. Somewhere, someone was burning leaves. The two maples in the library courtyard were the right red for tourist photographs. Halloween hadn't happened, but there was Halloween candy scattered across the walkway. An orange lollipop, shattered, was like a cubist sun.

He took me to a café, where he ordered us hot chocolate that was served ready-to-assemble: a wide-mouthed white cup of steaming milk on a saucer with a heaped spoonful of chocolate shavings and a miniature silver whisk for mixing.

"Alright?" he asked.

It was the most elegant thing I'd ever seen.

When the bill came, the cost of two hot chocolates was just shy of what I spent on groceries in a week. He stood and knotted his scarf, put on his coat, then tucked a bill under the vase at the center of the table.

"My treat."

My relief was physical.

"Wait," he said. He came back with a small silver bag, tipping it forward so I could see inside. There was a jar of chocolate shavings, a silver spoon, and a tiny whisk tucked into silver tissue paper. "Be gracious," he said, setting the bag in my hands. "Accept a gift."

At the bottom of the library stairs, which were slicked with a skim of ice, I worried for the man's balance, so I took my arm from his to let him take the rail. Unintentionally, I found myself near the top when he had barely begun the climb. I paused to wait.

From below he called, "If that skirt was any shorter, I'd say something about it."

I thought his comment was paternal: a reprimand. In the ladies' room, I patted cold water on my red cheeks and tugged my skirt down from waist to hips so the fabric rested at my knees.

My favorite place in the library was a storage room full of books whose repairs were unlikely ever to be made. In the library directory the room's designation was a number, but someone had hung a cedar shingle with Borning Room stenciled in serious black beside its door.

Borning is not, I think, a word found in the abridged version of the dictionary. In old houses, the borning room is off the kitchen, a small space kept warm by the cook stove on the other side of the common wall. When such things still happened at home, the borning room was where babies were birthed, and the sick were nursed until their end.

In the house where I grew up, there was a borning room tucked between the sitting room and kitchen. My mother used the space as an oversized closet. During mid-century renovations, the room had been overlooked: no electricity, no fixtures. To pick an outfit, my mother would turn on the lights in the sitting room and kitchen, then open the connecting doors.

I used to take a hand mirror and close myself inside to whisper *Bloody Mary, Bloody Mary*. Or I would *snick* the doors shut and, in the dark, push through the curtain of my mother's clothes. She kept them on a long wheeled rack, and I liked to pretend I had been forgotten, locked in a department store after closing, made to wait through the night. With the fabrics brushing my face, I would imagine reunions: how awful my mother would feel, the praise I would receive for being brave. Inhaling her faint smell, I would rub my face against her clothes, silky nylon and scales of sequins. Frightened and righteous, I whispered, "You can't just forget me."

After she left, my father phoned from the borning room to tell me he could smell my mother on the clothes she'd left behind. He was sobbing, "Tell me where she is. Where's my wife?"

"I don't know."

I thought he would shift to anger. Instead, he became sly, "I won't bother you again. I'm going."

I cried out "Wait!" I could picture it: the spattered walls, a cardigan of my mother's on the floor—pulled from its hanger by the wet weight of blood. But my father was breathing evenly in my ear. He hadn't lowered the phone. I thought: *He isn't going anywhere.*

"They'll bear *me* out the borning room door."

"Please stop." The heel of my hand was pressed to my heart to hold it in place.

"You'll be the one," he promised, "to find my body."

On the real bridge that Faulkner's fictional Quentin Compson jumped from, workers in quilted vests and hard hats wound red and white garland around the rails, making candy cane stripes. Glittery cutouts of golden bells and silver stars hung from the light posts. The river's surface had turned to slush. Snow fell, quiet and deep.

Inside the library, all but the emergency lights were off and the rugs were still rolled. The day-shift custodians wouldn't arrive for half an hour. I moved around the lobby turning on computers. I checked the night drop box. In the warren of empty cubicles behind the circulation counter, the man was waiting at my desk. In front of him was a narrow box tied with gold ribbon.

He pushed it toward me. "Open it."

Inside, wrapped in gold tissue paper, were leather gloves. A keyhole notch at the wrist showed fur lining. "I can't accept these."

He pushed up from the chair. "Can't you just be gracious?" Taking me by the shoulders, he sat me in the seat he had left. "Here—I'll show you how." He folded his hands femininely. In a falsetto he said, "Thank you. What a lovely gift. You do so much for me."

"I'm sorry," I said.

He thrust the box at my chest.

I tried again, "Thank you. You do so much for me."

"I do," he said. "I do a lot. You should be appreciative."

"I am."

"Are you?"

"I am."

Over fragrant cups of flowering tea, the man said, "I've become so fond of you." He touched my cheek. His thumb moved to my bottom lip. He pressed. The tip slipped inside. His skin tasted of cigarettes.

I turned my face away. Too hard, I set my cup into its saucer. Tea splashed the tablecloth. I said, "You're like a father to me."

"Really?"

"Yes."

Under the table, his hand found my knee. "I don't feel like a father."

I could not name the hot-cold sensation lurching through me: disgust or excitement? It was neither. It was both. I could not look up. A beautiful thing was happening in my tea cup: a jasmine blossom, sewn into itself, was unfurling.

It was another early morning, before the library opened, before anyone else arrived. The lights were still off, but the computers were on, and their screens had a lavender glow. I was on a wheeled stool, reshelving reserve books behind the circulation counter. Up on my toes, I tried to straighten the row. My balance was shaky; one of the casters on the stool was broken, and it shifted like a pony waiting for the moment to show off its underestimated animal self. Still, I was confident in the quiet and the near dark, balancing on one foot, straining up.

Had I fallen, I might've been hurt. I might've taken shelves down on top of myself, or split my head like a melon, but at the moment I wobbled I was steadied by a hand on my hip, another between my legs.

"No, no," he whispered against my back. He smelt of cigarettes and the clean cold outside. "Don't move." His rubbed his cheek against my sweater. "How long," he asked, "have you been waiting for me just like this?" The wire of his beard scratched through the layers of my clothes. "You look," he whispered, dragging a finger along the seam of my nylons, "positively crucified."

When I went to the house for the first time since my mother left, I discovered that something I had thought was a lie was the truth: the paintings *were* gone from the walls.

"My Mediterranean scenes," my mother called them. To me, they looked like nothing—pastel smears, a column maybe, the suggestion of coral sky and baby blue water, but she saw in them balcony views of a fig orchard. Where they'd hung were rectangles paler than the rest of the wall.

My father followed behind me. "I told you. She stripped the joint."

In the sitting room, the door to the record cabinet was open.

"I hope," he said, "you didn't want to listen to any Carole King."

"No."

"Because she took Carole King."

In the far wall, the door to the borning room was open. My mother, unless she was inside, had always kept it closed. Absently, I said, "I don't care about Carole King."

"You don't care?" The anger in my father's voice made me turn. I hadn't really looked at him until just then. His clothes fit like borrowed things. "We played Carole King at our wedding." His mouth kept pulling, never settling into an expression.

"Dad," I said, reaching out, but not touching. I could feel his trembling through the air.

He said, "I want to show you something."

In the laundry room clothes were piled on the floor. Whites had been separated from colors. The blue button-ups my father wore for his work were in their own pile, and so were the heavy canvas things he wore to work on his truck or around the yard. "You could come by," he said, "and *do* a little." His mouth pulled up then collapsed. "Since you care so much."

"I do," I said. "I will."

"I do," he mocked. "I will."

I listened to him walking away. I listened to him coming back. He wasn't large—he didn't fill the door. "You didn't even ask what I wanted for supper."

"You want me to make you supper?"

"I want a milk-poached egg and toast."

My arms were full of laundry. Chambray work shirts that smelled of old sweat. "Alright."

"Make the toast extra crisp."

I made him a milk-poached egg and dark toast. I served it to him on a tray in the sitting room because he was watching the news and didn't want to come to the table. When he complained the toast wasn't crisp enough, I made more. Before I left, I washed and dried the dishes. I hung out a load of laundry.

Laid out on the braided rug, my skirt shoved up, I was sweating, nauseous. The man wanted me to compliment his size by complaining of discomfort. I did. He provided narration; I spoke when prompted. He began, "You can barely handle this." I agreed; "I can't take it." "Yes you can. You like it." My sweater was twisted, cutting into the side of my neck. "You'll take it." "I'm taking it…"

A book trolley with a squeaking wheel rolled past his office door. I flinched. "It's locked," he said, heaving up into me. "Pay attention."

My phone began to ring. "I am. I like it," but I'd lost the plot. The phone trembled against my ribs, insisting. "Say," he said, "'you're too

much for me.'" He was running his thumbs across my cheeks. "Please"—
I realized I was crying—"it's too much."

Afterward, he offered to take me to lunch. "I don't know about you,"
he said, "but I worked up an appetite." He offered me his arm. "I'll take
you somewhere nice." He slapped my thigh, playful, rough, and sweet.
"You earned it."

At the restaurant, my hands had a tremor. I thought of tiny forks,
heavy spoons, rich sauces with too many vowels in their names. I thought
of the man's thick shoulders under my hands. I thought of his perfect
teeth against my throat. In the ice water there was a translucent cut of
cucumber. I ordered the special by pointing.

Flat on the floor, I'd missed a call from my father. Through lunch, I
waited for him to call again, to prove one missed call meant nothing—
hadn't I picked up all the others?—that he was all bluff, but the phone
stayed still as a dead thing.

When the man dismissed me, rather than return to the library, I
left for the house.

Early daffodils were breaking through the pebbled crust of the last
snow. On the bus, I passed bright beds of them, silk-yellow, newly burst
into bloom. The streets were sluiced with gray slush. Turning corners
the bus sent up tall waves of dirty water. On the sidewalk, people leapt
back too late. Under my seat a heater blew hot grit against my ankles. I
thought I would find my father's body.

Just through the door, I stood in the front hall trying to gauge the
quality of the air. Was it leaden? Did it have a pall of death? My slow
breaths, held and examined, identified nothing more than the coldness
and the silence, the odor of coffee and limes—and of cigarette smoke,
maybe coming from my own skin.

The sitting room was empty, tidied. Matching crocheted antimacas-
sars were centered on the arms of the sofa, another was draped neatly
across the back. A newspaper, disassembled, had been refolded and set
away on a side table. The door to the borning room was closed.

The shock waiting on the other side was the absence of a body. I knew the shapes in the corners by memory: the broken chairs stacked into a prickle-backed beast, the dented red dome of a charcoal grill, the pile of salvaged boards, the clam rake, the bushel basket of hinges and knobs. There was nothing there that didn't belong, but there was a change, a restoration: my mother's wheeled clothing rack was full.

In the kitchen, I found my father smoking in a chair pulled away from the table, shirtless, his pants on, but not zipped or buttoned. The fabric was open in a sloppy v, and I saw the soft fold of his penis and looked away. I thought *I cannot breathe*, but was breathing. I could taste the smoke from his cigarette.

On the counter there was a small cutting board holding pale wedges of lime and a paring knife. Beside the board was a second lime, whole, but skinned down to the pith, and in a tumbler at the edge of the sink its peel was twisted into a garnish called a horse's neck, which was what my mother always used to make fancy her gin-and-tonics.

Behind me the chair whined, adjusting as weight lifted from it, and then there was the slow *churrr* of my father zipping his fly. "Mom's out back," he said.

Then, I thought it was her body I would find.

On the patio, in her robe and unlaced winter boots, my mother stood with a cup of coffee. The steam rose around her face. Icicles on the eaves were melting at a steady drip, and on the clothesline, a half-dozen of my father's work shirts were hanging sodden. From the street beyond the fence came the normal noises of traffic and people, along with the dizzy gurgle of water tumbling into the downspouts. My mother didn't hear me.

When she turned, her face was flat calm, but shifted to a smile. "The gang's all here."

I could feel the ugliness of my reaction, the warped shaping of my mouth—twisting, jerking. Even in the freshness of the cold, I smelt cigarettes coming from my skin and from my mother's skin too. I thought I might cry, but my eyes were sapped.

"Don't be upset." My mother moved to take me in her arms. "Everything's fine."

For a moment, we stood chest to chest. I listened to the melt water running in the streets, the sound of the promise of renewal. The taste of smoke was in my throat. I pulled away.

"Look at you," my mother said.

I waited, wondering what she could see.

"Look at you, looking at me as if I've ruined your whole life." She upturned her mug, pouring coffee onto the uneven snow. "It's time to grow up." She moved toward the house. "You can't blame your parents for everything."

And I felt it keenly—how right she was.

Float

When my grandfather was dying, our dogs circled around him, moving like water coming to a boil, scrapping for the right to eat his vomit. A neighbor, performing a panicked approximation of CPR, hollered, "Bad!" at them between breaths, but they were shameless.

Outside, the ocean was spewing up into the street. Just before my grandfather had bent, then twitched, his whole body terrifying me with shuddering, before his head tipped back, and the air he drew rattled so hard inside him that it forced him to the floor, we were standing together at the window. He was worrying about my mother, his daughter, who was, right then, God only knew where.

"I wouldn't leave a dog out in that," he'd said.

A lobster, spit up in a violent spasm of water, was caught in the burlap that protected the roses. Over its mottled brown shell, a second skin was forming—a casing of thin, shining ice.

Gray-faced and defeated, the neighbor tried to cover my grandfather with a throw, but it was too short: from the shins down, he showed. I corralled the dogs into the bathroom, using my knees and pulling the skin on their backs. I locked them in. Later, high on anxiety, they chewed their way through the hollow-core door and ran room to room, their lips and tongues stuck with splinters. The big dog dripped fat red nickels while the little dog danced on hind-feet, whining, tracking the blood.

The weather calmed and the ambulance came, drawing more neighbors. What got to them, I think, was not that someone they knew had died, but all the red paw prints. Shoulder-to-shoulder in the foyer, I could hear them whispering: *Heart attack? Heart attack?*

I understood their disbelief.

At the hospital, a doctor brought me into a white room, empty except for the body. "You should touch him," the doctor said. I thought that he was teasing me, like a dare to step on a slug barefooted. I stood in the corner. I wouldn't go close.

While we waited for help to come, the neighbor apologized for giving up. He wiped his mouth with the back of his hand. We sat together, silent, on the floor. Beads of ice fell at an angle, knocking against the window glass. The neighbor moved to take my hand, but didn't. "Do you know—" He started, but had to stop and try again. "Where's—" He reached for my shoulder. All his gestures were hesitant, embarrassed, and embarrassing. Finally, he asked, "Your mother?"

I said, "I don't know." Then, to be sure he understood, "I wouldn't know."

His hand came up, and it was shaking just a little. He slid it across my hair until the strands were crackling under his palm, standing on end.

Before my grandfather took me, this is how we—my mother and I—lived, day-to-day: from deep sleep she would blink awake, hissing, snake-like. "Hhhss—" her hand fumbling across the bedside table for whatever it might find there—a cardboard coaster, a celery stalk swaddled in a napkin, an empty bottle with a label to strip clean from the glass. "Hhhss— Hhhss—" and she gave me whatever her blind hand found to keep me quiet and occupied then turned away and sank back into sleep, while the light straining through the curtains changed from gray to yellow to white. Sleeping hard, until a knock at the door, another, and another, and the knob turning in a half circle—the door locked and chained, always—one way then the other. She ignored everything beyond the bed. Then a face would press against the window, peering through the slit where the pulled blackout curtains failed to make a tight seam.

"Checkout." Someone, usually a man—his mouth wetting the glass, the oily print of a forehead, a nose, and a chin left behind. "It's ten," they would say, or eleven, or at some places, noon. "Let's go. Let's go," accompanied by the flat side of a fist pounding loud and reluctant. "Don't make me call somebody."

Days when the weather was mild enough for swimming, my grand-father woke me with a hand pressed between my shoulder blades. "Come on, then," as if I'd already kept him waiting. When I came down, he was at the stove, whisking sugar into a pan of milk and boiling water for cof-fee. The dogs paced tight circles around his legs, pushing against him, eager. The three of them had been up for hours.

He served me breakfast, milky coffee and toast with smoked tinned fish, then let the dogs lick the crumbs and oil off his fingers. Depending on the month, the time exactly and the tide, when it had last rained, and when the sun would rise, the light was blue, or green freckled gray, or the faintest foggy red. "Come on, then," he said, but to the dogs, and they sat still for him so he could slip his hand under each of their collars to check the fit.

When the sun went down, feral dogs started howling bloody-mur-der, coming together in packs on the beach. My grandfather told me they had been abandoned as puppies—whole litters thrown overboard, or off the bridge, but not bagged-up, or bagged-up, but not weighted-down. Those that managed the swim back to land became the strays that ran wild through the damp streets at night, overturning garbage cans and killing whatever they could catch—chickens, and cats, and mild-tempered guard dogs left out on chains.

"Admirable nuisances," my grandfather called them as he lined his sights. Though he worried our dogs would slip their collars and be mis-taken for feral and shot, he never hesitated in killing a stray. He kept his rifle ready, loaded, on the top shelf of the pantry, a quick step from the back stairs.

In secret, I pretended I was the special one who could tame the strays with love. Then one summer, playing alone on the rocks, I caught a stray distracted. It did not see me, did not run. I watched it dunk its head into a tide-pool and thrash. With my best care, moving slow and quiet, I eased up almost close enough to touch its yellow fur. When the stray raised its head, there was a small, green crab delicately pinched between its teeth.

I thought: how wonderful, how perfect, how very much like a story with wild little children living parentless in the woods and keeping beasts for pets. I thought: I could do *that*; the yellow dog could be tamed to be mine, loyal only to me, could dig us a den and hunt our meals.

As I watched, the stray flipped its head back, tossed and caught the crab with a wet crunch, and in the moment between, its mouth wide open, I saw the fat, flat ribbon of a thriving parasitic worm burrowing through its gum.

Sometimes we found a dog, collarless, dead on the beach. Time in the water bloated them, left them bald, turned their skin smooth and blue.

When I was still little and life with my grandfather was new, there was a time I said, "Poor thing. Poor thing," pointing at a dead dog on the sand.

He took my arm and walked me to the body. With the toe of his boot, he turned it to show the belly—the black swell of embedded tick heads, red-ringed with infection. "Poor thing?" I remember his grip was too tight. He used a stick to show the hole a bullet had made—right through. "Living," he said, "they suffer."

Already, flies were filling the dog's dead eyes, maggots tumbling from the slackened ring of its anus. Our dogs sniffed around the body, hackles up. My grandfather reprimanded them away and we moved on.

After I was fed my breakfast, we swam, and we swam side by side. The big dog paddled behind us and the little one ran along the sand. All the way to the end of the spit, and then we left the water. "That's good," he said. "That's miles." We walked back toward the cove, throwing sticks for the dogs, calling them when they ran too far ahead.

He told me stories. Often they started, "Your mother." Often he told me things without my ever asking.

"She wasn't a brave girl—not like you are." He threw a stick into the water. The big dog plunged after it. The little one barked. We watched the roll of the waves, the stick pulling away from the dog's grasping mouth. "She thought it would swallow her up. 'That's why you have to know,' I told her."

In pieces—that's how my mother learned to swim, a body part at a time. My grandfather held her under the arms and dipped her, squirming, knee-deep. Pressed her to her belly on the sand and told her to put her chin at the edge of the water and every so often a wave would fold harder than the ones before and slap across her face.

"What did she do?"

"She cried, but she had to learn."

One summer, when my mother was still a baby, a storm came in red across the water, the sky sizzling with lightning and tipped four kids in their aluminum boat, and then a full day later—as men stabbed gaffs between the rocks, downpoking for the bodies—the ocean offered them up again, whole and breathing, with pruney fingertips and toes.

My grandfather was an islander first, a sailor second. The soles of his feet were tattooed against drowning—a chicken on one, a pig on the other. In shipwrecks, livestock small enough for cages bobbed, buoyed along the waves, waiting on a lucky current to beach them safely on some shore. By the time I knew him, the color of the tattoos had distorted, and under a layer of callus their lines were not clean, but he still believed that knowing how to swim could save a life.

Days when it was raining, the big dog stretched out across my bed. Both of us were warned against tracking mud, against wet footprints on the patterned parquet in the hallway, and catching chills. The dog dreamed of swimming, flexing its webbed feet, paddling against the duvet. Sometimes, I lay beside it, hands curved into scoops, practicing when to turn my face, when to stroke and when to breathe.

"Next time," my mother said. "Tell him to let me have you. We'll go to the beach. I'll watch you swim."

I did, but she drove inland to a house with cars parked on the lawn. "Say I'm your babysitter," she said.

In the backyard, men sat in canvas beach chairs, drinking beer. The air smelled of mildew and septic tank and pine pitch. A teenager in headphones was stationed at a rusty propane grill. He pointed with a spatula, "Hamburger? Hotdog?"

A man came around the corner of the house, took my mother by the waist and lifted her. She screamed and laughed. A dog barked. Somewhere, a baby was crying. From the beach chairs, men cheered. The man holding her loosened his grip.

"Who's this?" he asked, as my mother landed unsteady, her hands held out for balance. She didn't answer him.

Another man came around the corner. He held a big pot to his chest. "We're putting crayfish on." He shouldered the boy with the spatula away from the grill. When he set the pot over heat—*taktaktak*—a hundred startled tails slapping against metal.

I reached for my mother and she caught my hands. "What did I say?" She pushed me back.

One of the beer drinkers pulled himself up from his chair. He came toward us. "What's this?" he looked down at me. He was bony-thin, but had a hanging belly, sun-pinked, covered with curling hair. He pointed with his can of beer. "You know a trick? You know a little song?"

Another man, running across the lawn, slowed, slung my mother over his shoulder and kept going.

"Whadaday teach you at school?" The man stepped closer. "The Spanish alphabet?"

I stepped back.

"I've got a kid who knows the whole Spanish alphabet." He tapped the beer can against my chest. "Show me something."

The boy from the grill came out the front door and down the steps. He was still wearing headphones. As he walked by, the man with the belly caught him by the shoulder of his T-shirt. He pulled the boy close, roughly, flattening his beer can against the boy's back. "And where the fuck do you think you're going?"

"Nowhere," the boy said, looking down.

The man with the belly yanked the boy's headphones off and threw them. "Alright then." He shoved the boy away.

Behind the man's back, the boy mimed a jack-in-the-box with his hands, turning an invisible crank until his middle finger sprang up.

Sometimes my mother and I were friends. She'd have a little gift for me, pass it hidden between her hands. "Guess," she said. She held out fists, "Which one." Not always, I don't think, but often, her knuckles were raw, scabbed, split, or festering.

I watched her once, when her hands were swollen, bite the plastic nub from a bobby pin and use the little rough bit of metal underneath to puncture the infection.

"Like this now." She showed me where to squeeze and how to coax the pus out.

With her gifts, she'd say, "Pick," her hands in front of her. "You have to pick."

I chose a hand by touching it and then she pressed something from her palm into mine—a paper-wrapped rosette of motel soap, a cocktail umbrella that opened and closed, three withering red cherries on a tiny plastic sword.

I don't remember crossing the white room, but I did. Two fingertips to his chest, my grandfather was not as cold or as warm as he should have been. It was like touching something unfamiliar in the dark—that kind of wrongness. My hand jerked away.

The doctor said, "Take your time."

When I was very small, my grandfather held me against him, my skin to the same bare skin at my fingertips, and through my body I felt him draw a heavy breath. I stiffened in his arms; knowing better did not make me any less afraid of the water around us.

He said, "The body naturally floats," then released his hold, dropping me off the dock's end.

My mother said, "You know what he said to me? He said, 'I wish to God that something happened to you.' He said that. He did. He said, 'When you were really little—I wish it; something really awful—so bad I could say, It's not her fault she's this way she is.'" She had me by the wrists. "He said that to me. He did. Can you believe that?"

I wouldn't look at her. We were standing in the mud-thickened water below a sea-heather bloom. Through the grit I could see half a dozen horseshoe crabs gathering at her feet. There were none around mine. She was wearing lime-green espadrilles with crisscross laces that cut into her calves.

"Look at this," she said, pointing down. A horseshoe crab mounted her foot, carapace fluttering.

I looked away.

"Everybody wants to fuck me!" She was laughing, shaking with it.

I could hear my heart beating, the *swoop-whoosh* of blood in my ears.

"There's nothing wrong with me. Everybody wants me. Even the crabs want some." Leaning forward she clapped her hands and lost her balance and I had to grab at her waist to keep her from falling.

In the chokecherry outside the room that used to be my mother's, my grandfather hung a wind-chime made from bottles washed up on the beach. Rarely did they make it ashore whole, but he had a collection. The light filtered through them, watery against the walls. For me the room was soft green. When it was still my mother's, my grandfather took her to Aubuchon Hardware and stood with her at the wall of paint samples.

"Show me how," I asked him. "Show me how she picked."

He would bend to me, lifting me under the arms, holding me high, facing the blank wall of the kitchen. In the store, the pastels were at the very top of the display, color-cards darkening downward. She had the room painted petal pinks—for years and years. Below the bedroom window, low on the wall, like a geode halved, was a circle of nested colors, where, when he re-painted, my grandfather always left a ring of the shade before, the earliest at the center, and the outermost—her last pick—against the green that was mine.

"She liked pink."

"She did," he said, "and lilac."

Sitting on the bedroom floor, I could touch each color she had chosen. I could say, "This was her favorite. She liked this best."

"Can we do that? Can we paint my room for spring?" I only asked him the one time. Outside, snow was melting, filling the streets with water. On the beaches, sand frozen into wind-shaped ridges that curved like wings, was softening, crumbling grain by grain.

"No," he said, "we can't."

"What if I want it pink?"

"No." He snapped his fingers. The big dog came to him.

"Why?"

He played with the fringe of fur along its ears. "No." He clicked his tongue and the dog set its head on his knee.

"Why not?" In the kitchen the light was the brightest of anywhere in the house and I could see the white in his hair, at his temple and behind his ear. "Why not, Papa?" The dog's muzzle was going white too. "Why not?"

He looked at me. "I'll slap your smart mouth is 'why not.'"

My mother leaned toward me when she spoke, "Does he try and feed you fish?" She twisted her hair into a tail and laid it over her shoulder. "Does he try and feed you little smoked fish on toast?" Sometimes, she forgot my age. She didn't know how to talk to me. "Does he? Does he make you eat that awful, awful stuff?"

Yes, he did, and little cups of coffee half full with sweet, scalded milk, and if I ever, by mistake, forgot at dinner and lifted my fork before he had lifted his, he looked at me and said, "Who taught you manners?" Then, he took my plate away, but made me sit and watch him while he ate.

"Oh, I know," she said. "I know. I know." She had a plastic bag full of make-up, emptied out, spread across the backseat of the car. She drew around her lips, filled them in too heavily. Sometimes she kissed me rather than blot the color on the edge of a dirty shirt and left the fruity grease of her lipstick on my mouth. "Me," she said, "I only drank ginger ale. I would only eat butter shortbread cookies." She touched my face, my hair. "Did he give you any money? Should we go and get you whatever you want?"

We went across the bridge for early-bird dinner at the cafeteria in the department store in town. Only old people ate there. They served buttermilk and soft things on toast. I wanted a hotdog, but my mother ordered us Welsh rarebit to share.

She said, "I'm not chewing anything." One side of her mouth was swollen and shiny. Her canine tooth was broken, jagged-edged. "I need a nail file to flatten this off." She emptied her purse on to the table.

When she was little, my mother picked her dresses from the store upstairs and rode the elevator up and down, over and over while a seamstress made adjustments so they would fit her perfectly. I asked her, "Tell me about the elevator?"

She lifted her glass of water, tried to drink. "My goddamn mouth hurts." She set the glass back down, fished out an ice cube, and slipped it under her top lip. "You tell me when the food comes." She folded her arms and put her head down on the table.

"Don't," I touched the part of her hair. "Sit up. Everyone's looking."

It wasn't once that my mother came to the house late, unsteady in her heels. If we had ever fought I would not have accused, "That time—" One night or another, with the sun nearly down, but light enough left to throw her shadow up the stairs and darken where I sat waiting, she staggered toward me with her arms held out.

"Look who's here," she said. "Look who I've found."

When I hugged her, the skin of her back was hot against my arms, tightening with a sunburn that hadn't the time yet to go red. With our bodies close there was the slow smell of smoke in her hair, tomato juice on her breath. Through her dress I could feel lines of her bikini—the bulge of the knot at her spine, the metal rings at the bones of her hips. At her neck, the knot was askew. Strands of hair were tied into it.

I could hear my grandfather inside, moving forward through the house. "Let's go," I said.

It was always too late. Whatever was planned, it was too late. "A day at the beach," she said. "I want to see you swim."

"But it's dark."

She didn't listen. "We'll go to the beach. Oh. Oh. We'll have so much fun. I'll watch you." We passed the one-room summerhouses, their porches lit, the bulbs circled by gray moths. "You can show me how you swim."

We stopped at the market. The bottles stowed under the car seats rolled forward and clacked one against the other.

One night—the three of us, together in a car. My grandfather was driving, and I could feel my mother in the seat in front of me, how she was curled up with her face against the window. I knew the secrets to faking sleep—not to squeeze the eyelids tight, to keep the mouth a little open, to take each breath slowly, to make each exhale the same.

I felt the shift from gravel that groaned softly under the tires, to the near silent sigh of sand. I could hear my own careful breathing. We angled forward, starting down a low dune onto the flat stretch of beach. The bottles my mother had hidden under the seats rolled forward. *Clack.*

"You break my heart," my grandfather said. "If that's any kind of proof you're loved, you break my goddamn heart."

So late in the day, all that was left was fake-crabmeat on a roll. "It's good," I said. In the light, my mother's skin was dark and cracked as a cricket's wing. "We can share."

"Did he give you money?"

"Yes." And dimes and nickels for a payphone.

The boy at the register looked up. "Hey, now," he said, shaking his head. Tacked to the beam beside him was a Polaroid of my mother with her hair skinned back. Above it was a note. *No Checks.*

She pointed to the bottles on the shelves behind him. Her other hand was curled around the back of my neck. "I have cash."

Once, in some summer when I was very small, my grandfather sat in an Adirondack chair on a sunbather's deck built out into the smooth water of the cove, and I lay on my back, under his feet, tracing the animals that seemed trapped inside his skin. A ragged dog came out from the weeds with its head held low. Its body—its whole, entire body—was marked with open circles, each one seeping pus, each one ringed with bruise. I watched it crawl into the shadows under the deck, and through a crack between the boards, lay down heavily in the mud.

"Papa," I said.

And he lifted me up onto his lap. "Shh."

The doctor came toward me slowly. "You have to trust there's no more anyone can do." He took my hand in his cold hand and laid it lightly on my grandfather's arm. "So you know what's gone." Wrapped around mine, his fingers were steady, kind pressure.

I asked, "What's going to happen?"

"To your grandfather?"

Down the hall, in another room, my mother was wailing. "You have to save my dad. You have to save my dad." Her voice was so loud it tore.

"To me."

"Go on," my mother said. "I'm watching."

The sand was pitted where each pellet of hail had struck then melted away, but the water was tepid. I wanted her to call me back to shore, to her, so I swam straight out. Past the wave break the water was black. I turned and floated, watching her small and glowing on the beach.

My mother.

Did she lift her hand, as if to shield her eyes, as if she was looking hard out at the water?

I don't think she did.

I know she didn't call for me. I ducked under. Further out, the water smoothed. I could feel the cold of real depth under me, licking at the soles of my feet. On the beach, she was something white and moving, nothing recognizable. I did not call to her. I watched her go.

Worry

At the end of a dirt turn-around, a dog walker loses hold of his shepard and watches, helpless, as it pelts away. *Fingersnap*—that quick, it's out of sight in the trees, disappearing through speckled alders that grow down a steep embankment to flourish in swampy land below.

The dog walker calls, "You! You!"

But it's already going at something. Sound carries. Digging. Whining. The man rolls his pant cuffs and plunges down the slope. More sliding than walking, he leaves behind a flattened swath. As he skids toward even ground the air fills with something white and weightless lifting on the wind.

It isn't snow; a float trails across his cheek without a sting. A bit catches in his hair. He pulls it free. Rubbing it between two fingers—*soft*—he makes a quick determination: down. Cursing, he flicks it away. Cold mud slops his cuffs. Forced to move slowly, he swears again with feeling.

He expects the dog to have a bird.

What he discovers is a child.

A girl.

Locked in the ice, her pale hair is spread all around her, and the dog, digging at her narrow back, shredding the nylon shell of her jacket, churns curls of down into the air.

They meet like anybody meets. Pressed, he could not say for certain where he was, or what it was he was doing the first time that he saw her, or even what first words were exchanged between them. (He would place equal bets on *hey* and *hello*.) Through common coincidence, small town eventualities, their paths cross and cross until they are entangled. On occasion, they drink beer in the same pine paneled bar. In the back, he plays darts against himself. Near the front window, bathed in white winter light, she sits at a high top table, eating maraschino cherries from a little porcelain bowl.

They arrive at the same places a slivered moment apart and end up passing through doorways like a couple—as if they've run out together to pick up milk and bread they'll share—though they are still strangers. From afar—as the expression goes, though often there is little physical distance between them—he admires her.

Once she pulls into a driveway behind him at the instant he's cutting his motor. They make small talk walking to the door of the house of a mutual acquaintance. The porch is bedecked in lights, pulsating with holiday cheer. It's brutally cold. His fingers are still curled, locked into the shape they took around the steering wheel. Needles of snow prickle against his skin, and he's hurrying to be out of the weather, and her nose is red from the cold, and she's sniffling, and the colored lights blinking in the bushes and wrapped around the porch rail splash her face unflatteringly with green and blue and red, and all her blonde-white hair is tucked up under a fisherman's beanie. He doesn't realize until they are inside and separated that she is the woman whose proximity has, for some time, stupefied him.

In his throat the missed opportunity lodges as physical pain. Like a fishbone, it's sharp-edged when he swallows.

A dozen small groups of conversation have formed. He floats, flotsam, nothing to add. In the far corner, she's dancing by herself, eyes closed, twisting her hips and shaking her hair. She's crowned herself with a loop of garland. When she shimmies, her sweater pulls up, showing the tender declivity at the base of her spine. He understands that only her looks save her from embarrassment.

Weeks later, on the sidewalk passing the beauty salon he pauses to breathe in its warm, chemical smells, thinking of his mother, not long gone. When he was a child, she would treat herself by letting another woman wash and style her hair. She hemmed and hawed before the

appointment, "It's not necessary," ready to cancel. Practical, hardwork-
ing, she saved her pennies for him. But when she allowed herself, she
would return from the salon lustrous, as if in the process of a shampoo
and set, something inside her had been polished.

Breathing deep, he sees what he has not before: beyond the window,
the blonde sits in the first chair, her pale hair wet down her back. He
offers an uncertain wave.

She pushes up and crosses to the door. The bells on the handle ring
high and bright. Leaning out into the cold, her white hair steams as the
black smock catches a current of air and swells around her.

"Hey—" he begins. "Hello."

She tips her head, considering, "I know you?" Her hair falls around
her shoulders like water streaming off of ice.

"No," he says, then, "Yes?" and names the bar, the host of the party,
the little grocery where he has stood behind her in the late night checkout line.

"Okay," she says. "Yeah," and she smiles, flicking a hand in a wave
before ducking back inside.

Minutes, hours, days, a week. It stays with him: that smile, the liquid whiteness of her wet hair, the off-whiteness of her teeth. And then,
idling at a stop sign, no one behind him, waiting for the car lighter to
pop, she—the blonde—passes on the sidewalk dressed in scrubs only
this-much lighter than her hair.

A moment of insight: she's a nurse's aide, mopping up after the aged.
"Bedpan Brigade," his mother used to say, ironing her own worn white
uniform. "It's not glamorous, but it's good." Good work, she meant,
work that paid, and good work, to care for others. She was on the three
to eleven shift—slopped, as he remembers it, in misery and fluids. He
was always in bed when she came home, always awake, lying wide-eyed,
trying to see past the dark, waiting for the barely groan of the door
swinging in, the thump of the deadbolt after it closed. She would come
to his bedside. "You're up." Her soft hand cupped his forehead. "I can
tell." Sometimes he would get up to put the leftovers of the dinner she
had made for him in the microwave then sit across from her, silent,

while she ate. Sometimes, she would smile, reach across the table, and squeeze his hand.

He rolls down the window. The blonde is close enough to hear him call. He wouldn't have to shout. Should he offer her a ride? In the wind, her hair is going wild. She wraps an arm around her head to lash it down. He begins to coach himself, to practice turns of phrase. Should he call her Miss? He knows her name, but does not have a reason to; they've never been formally introduced. Would she remember him from the salon? Would she think it's strange, his turning up again? His knowing her name? It could be, he worries, the wrong move. Too familiar. *Excuse me, Miss*—he tests it out. *Miss?* Incrementally, she grows smaller. Heated, the lighter pops. He ignores it.

She becomes a white smear. The lighter's metal coil has cooled to useless. He depresses it again. Behind his eyes, he can feel every lurch and throb of his heart.

Yet—

Miracles happen?

It happens.

They are in bed together, where they have been for the majority of two days. And over the course of that time, she has become his girlfriend. And now, she is weakly insistent about a need to leave.

The night before, he showered with the door open so he could watch her through the frosted glass, a long, white figure reclining, warped as if under moving water. Into the shower spray he said to himself things he wanted to say to her. "You've filled me," he whispered. "You're everything," the hot water spilling into his mouth.

A towel around his hips, he had asked her to stay again. She did. The night is past. The mid-morning sun glares white off fresh snow. Their most critical business is finished. She's laid on her belly. He straddles her. Into a hank of her damp hair, he's braiding a dozen tiny braids.

Behind her ears, she smells poached. Mild, soft, and edible.

"I gotta go," she says. She squirms. "Off."

Already, there is so much between them. Like: he can do a near perfect imitation of her. Her *got*. Her *yeah*. She'll give it right back. "Verily," she'll say. "Indeed." He's objected, "I don't talk like that," though he understands the seed of her impression.

"Yeah," she says. "But yeah though. You do."

Now, he starts another tiny braid and asks, "You have plants to water?"

"No." She rolls away. Her hair slides through his fingers. "But I got a kid."

He has seen, but not asked about the thin white scars puckering her stomach. He knows he should not say what he does, but does. "I have room."

She twists, looking at him sharply.

He makes an attempt. "I respect," he begins, "that you're a mother."

Her expression becomes appraising.

The first night, while the blonde was in the bathroom, water running, but not loud enough to cover the dizzying separation of zipper teeth as she undressed behind the closed door, he crept across the bedroom to the dresser where his mother's urn had sat since its collection. Dusting, he would wipe it down, but never touched it with his bare skin. In the bathroom, the pipes shuddered. He pulled his t-shirt out from his belly, covered his hands, and lifted the urn. Through the thin fabric it was cold and heavy.

The water pipes stuttering to stillness prompted him to move. On the other side of the bathroom door she was riffling through her pocketbook. A cosmetic case or a pillbox opened and shut with a pair of sharp clicks. Like a child sneaking, he moved on tiptoes down the narrow hall. In the living room, he lifted the urn onto the mantle above the fireplace.

The blonde, slim and white as a taper, stepped into the hall, hands held out. "Wanna," she grinned, "come with me?"

His hand comes to rest at the center of her back. It rides the gentle waves of her breathing. Over her shoulder, she watches him with eyes that are barely a color at all. Pressing a cheek alongside his hand, he listens to air pulled and pushed by her lungs, absorbs the warmth of her skin. Hoping, imagining this—*them*—all the time, he says, "I like mothers."

She laughs, "Oh yeah?"

He is honest, kissing along her spine, "I don't like to be alone."

He buys a kit—a girl's bedroom in a bag. There is a pink comforter and two pink pillow cases, a dust ruffle, a thin rug shaped like a crown, and plastic decals to stick on the wall. P-R-I-N-C-E-S-S. He arranges the letters in a line behind the camp cot he's brought in from the shed. A proper bed is not an option just now. All his furniture has been moved to his mother's room, and all her furniture, to the curb before he collected her ashes. All of it was infused with her smell, her smell overlaid with the smell of her sickness: powder, antiseptic cream, cloves, and a sweet, subtle rot. He couldn't tolerate that ghost of her.

The stick-on letters are crooked. He peels them down and tries to make them straighter. He makes up the cot. The sheets are too big. He tucks them tightly around the mattress, but they rumple and billow. The comforter drags on the floor. He can admit it doesn't look good. He rearranges the rug, moving it to the center of the room. No difference.

From the window he can make out distant children, swathed head to toe in primary colors, playing on the hill. They are lifting handfuls of snow and hurling them above their heads. Coming down, sunlight turns the flakes to a shower of glitter.

The girl might be five or six, older than that, or younger. He is not familiar with children. She has a narrow shape, rectangular, without any indentation or outward curve. Her age remains a mystery. She gives him no hint of how he should proceed. Because it is his impression that formality makes children feel important, like one of the adults, he says, "Hello," bending, a hand extended. "How do you do?"

Immobile—a shy child?—she stares at him, mute. This, he treats as permission to look her over more thoroughly. She has curly hair, darker than her mother's, but still strikingly light, blonde enough to be nearly white. Her romper is sizes too small. It strains across her chest and nips at her crotch. Vaguely, he is embarrassed.

He wonders, Does she dress herself? And dressed as she is, does she go un-corrected? But it isn't his place. He is not her father. Though, as he must have had a father, so must she, this girl—somewhere. The thought rises, a cresting wave of panic, then folds and fades back. He has seen no sign of this other. Not hide nor hair.

Hand ignored, he tries a new approach; in the girl's arms is a custardy smelling rabbit doll. He tweaks a drooping whisker. "Who's this fine fellow?" He believes he's being a sport, but the girl pulls away, drawing the doll close to her chest, giving him an odious look.

He asks, "How old are you?"

She parrots the question back, "How old are you?"

His girlfriend, coming from the car, claps her child across the back of the head. "Don't be a piss-ant." She continues to the house, but turns on the bottom step, "Say, 'I love you.'"

Simultaneously, they do—the girl and him, both speaking up at her on the stairs.

His girlfriend laughs. The wind stirs her white hair. She shifts her hold on the box in her arms and brushes strands from her face. Looking to her daughter, she points at him. "Tell ma's friend," she says. "Say, 'I love you,' to him."

He feels his cheeks flushing, and for grounding allows himself to take in the muscular play of his girlfriend's ass—he has held that in his hands, his touch encouraged—mounting the final stairs, before returning his attention to the child. "You don't have to," he says. "You shouldn't say that unless you want to."

The girl lifts her eyes from the rabbit's fur.

"I'm—" He uses his hands to flash the amount. "Twenty-seven." Isn't that something children do?

The girl is distinctly unimpressed. She answers without looking up from between the rabbit's ears. "Nine."

"Nine?" It's good. Isn't it? It's a good thing, that they're talking? "That's quite big." He clears his throat. "Nine."

The girl loosens her grip on the rabbit to extend one slight hand, soft and blue veined, more delicate than a salamander's belly. Cautiously, he shakes it.

His mother left the house to him. It's his to keep up. Today is windows. The inside of each pane is already done. With a bucket of hot water and vinegar, newspaper under his arm to wipe the glass clean, he works his way around. There's a deceptive hint of spring in the air. He's gloveless. His jacket is unzipped. Still, steam is rising off the bucket in a white column. An early nor'easter is forecasted for later in the week. Anticipated: two feet of snow. Up on the hill, children are sledding. A dog chases them down and runs ahead on the hike back up. At the top it turns to bark.

He comes to the girl's window. Once this was his room. Inside, she and her mother are dancing arm in arm. *I'll come back*, he thinks, but stays. He watches them move out from a close, slow sway to grip one another by the wrists. Next comes laughing and spinning. Lunatics. He smiles. Were the girl any smaller, she'd be lifted off the floor. He sets the bucket in the snow. The force of their momentum is pulling them apart now. Together, whipping in a circle, they're shouting a countdown, "One!—Two!—Three!" They let go. His girlfriend stumbles back. The girl goes flying. She crashes into the camp cot, and it, of no substance at all, folds, going down with her in a jumble. He raps on the glass. His girlfriend straightens. Her face is pink. She comes to the window. A gesture with her hands asks, *Well?*

He claps, making a circle in the air as he does. Something picked up from the girl: *A round of applause*. Behind her mother, she pops up, the woman in miniature. Like a scrubbed apple, she shines. Her wild, whitish hair is everywhere. His reflection is held in the glass between mother and daughter. From his perspective, they look almost like a photograph of a family in a frame. The girl disrupts the thought, startling him by blowing a kiss. A beat late, he raises an open hand to catch it. His girlfriend snatches the kiss from the air.

At night, down the hall, he can hear the girl turning on the cot. The springs of the frame compress in a long whine then labor to re-achieve their height as she rolls from belly to back, back to belly. Fidgety—if she sleeps at all. In bed, he listens to the girl moving for hours. Beside him, his girlfriend sleeps soundly. He wonders, touched by uncertainty, how? Aren't mothers meant to be tuned to the frequency of their children? He thinks of his mother in the doorway of his room, "I know you're awake," and slips from bed. His girlfriend sleeps on, undisturbed.

The girl's door is open. She is sitting up on the cot, her back to him, head bent, using the light from the streetlamp to study something in her lap.

"You should be sleeping."

The girl's thin shoulders jump. She scrambles with the bedding. The sheets are rumpled on the floor, but she snaps up a blanket and swirls it across the mattress in an attempt at concealment. He's caught her at something.

"What have you got?"

The girl hunches down, shaking her head. He pulls the covers back. Beside the rabbit doll, his mother's urn dents the bare mattress. He grabs it up. Against his skin, it's cold. It's heavy. Having forgotten its weight, he must adjust his hold. His palms feel scorched. It's amazing the girl didn't drop it.

He brings the urn to his chest. "This isn't yours."

"I'm sorry," the girl whispers, then undoes her apology completely, "I only wanted to see!"

"You wanted to *see*?"

The girl tips her face up. Her lower lip is trembling. She bites down until it stills. The cot springs shift continuously. She moves with a gentle weave, a little sailor on a deck. Her expression, resigned and ready for punishment, unsettles him.

So she will understand the enormity of her wrongdoing, he tells her, "This is my mother." Then he waits. And waits. Fat snowflakes scatter shadows on the wall. The P decal is peeling away. Shifting the urn to the crook of his arm, he smooths the letter flat with his thumb. The girl has become, again, mute.

As he turns to go she scrambles from the cot, throwing herself against him, skinny arms locking his waist. "I only wanted to see." Her face is stricken, wet. For a moment he stays as he is. The girl's hold tightens then drops loose. She steps back, watching him warily. "I'm sorry."

He sets the urn in the doorway. There is a film of cold, like a first frost, over his palms. He rubs them up and down his shirtfront and crouches in front the girl. She curves a tentative palm around his neck. He lets her climb into his arms and attempts to comfort, "There, there," patting her narrow back.

Soon, she becomes a lax warm weight against his chest. As he moves to deposit her, the state of the cot registers. Knotted blanket. Sheets on the floor. He lays her on the bare mattress then goes about the slow and careful work of making the bed around her. Cupping the back of her head, he tries to slip her pillow into place, but catches her hair, accidentally pulling. She blinks at him. He offers her the rabbit doll. She curls around it, asleep again.

He cannot resist an urge: hiking the blanket higher, he tucks its edges in, protection for her pale little body against the cold.

He comes in through the mudroom to a scene: his girlfriend with a hairbrush held above her head—the beginning or end of a tremendous swing. The girl is on her knees, arms held stiff in front her. On one hand, the knuckles are split. There's a little blood, bright, dappled on the floor.

His girlfriend surges toward him. Palms facing out, his hands fly up, fingers spread. *Stay away.* He does not think about the gesture. It happens on its own. His girlfriend pauses, setting the brush on the tabletop, moving her hands to her hips. "She started it. You don't know how bad she can be."

While his attention is on her mother, the girl makes a move. Her small hand captures his wrist, pulling. Using burrowing force, she works to interlace their fingers. Her skin is chilled and soft. She tugs. When he bends toward her, she whispers up, "You can be on my side."

He is surprised to find himself sincerely moved. The girl *likes* him. Well—it's possible that he likes her too. So fine: this is not the first fight between mother and daughter, just the first this bad, the first with this sort of punishment, and he'll act as referee. He looks down at the girl, meaning to say something kind, and catches her flashing a grin of triumph at her mother.

His girlfriend begins to holler, "See! See! You see what she's like?"

"It's alright," he says. "Let's—"

"Jesus," his girlfriend says, "you like her. You think she's cute? Well, she's getting dark. She isn't half so blonde already."

The girl turns her face into his ribs. He shifts away because her breath tickles. "What?" Genuinely, he is confused.

With both hands, his girlfriend grabs her daughter by the head, fingers scrabbling to part tangled curls. "See," she tilts the girl's head forward and back.

"Don't be so rough."

"Look," his girlfriend runs a fingernail along the child's part where the hair is darker, "she's dirty blonde. You like blondes? She won't be."

He puts his hands over hers and lifts them gently from the girl's head.

His girlfriend squeezes his fingers. "She ain't blonde much longer."

"Hey," he squeezes back. "Hey," uncertain what to say.

He has a memory of his mother tipping over an invisible edge. They were in this kitchen and he was just a boy. He has forgotten what provoked her, what caused her to club him with sloppy fists, crying, "Just— Just— Just—"

He squeezes his girlfriend's hands again. "It's hard. I understand."

Now, from the far side of the kitchen the girl watches them with the little pearls of her baby teeth bitten into her bottom lip.

He and his girlfriend are on the couch. She is on her side, her white-blonde head in his lap. On the floor, between his spread feet, the girl and her rabbit doll are looking through a field guide for identifying plants. Lost in the woods, what would poison and what could nourish?

"Pinecones?" The girl asks. "True or false? Could I live off pinecones?"

"Why," he jokes, "are you planning on running away?"

"Don't I wish," his girlfriend says.

The girl goes silent for a moment, but cannot help herself: when she comes to a gruesome photo of an eruption of blisters, she pipes up again. "Oh my god," she holds the book up over her head, the pages facing him. "This is what poison sumac'll do."

"Stop," her mother says. "Cut it out," but her tone is mild.

The pitch in the pine logs in the woodstove pops. He is weaving his girlfriend's hair into a fisherman's knot. The heat is making one side of him too hot, but he doesn't want to move. Earlier, in the kitchen, he and his girlfriend washed and dried the dishes together. Each time he handed her a plate, a glass, a fork, she pecked him on the lips.

The rabbit doll's fatty, custard-y smell carries. He puts a bare foot on the girl's back. "Somebody needs a bath."

"Not it."

"Not you," he laughs. "Monsieur Lapin, there."

The girl's expression is aghast.

What? "What?" He has no clue.

From his lap, his girlfriend answers sleepily, "It's—"

"*He*," the girl corrects.

"—stuffed with sawdust."

With adult seriousness the girl explains, "He'd come apart." The field guide forgotten, she clutches the doll protectively.

"I didn't know." He makes a show of shaking his head. "I'm sorry."

And with that, everything is righted. The girl relaxes, shifting to her belly, tucking the rabbit carefully under her chin as she returns to the book.

He plays with his girlfriend's hair. The girl turns pages. Her small, cold feet drum gently on his shins. "Oh my gosh." The girl thrusts the book back at him. In full glossy color is a small boy who looks as if raw eggs are sprouting from the skin of his chest and arms.

"Stay away from that one."

She grins back at him. "Do you know what did this?"

"No."

"But, do you *want* to know?"

"Sure."

"Ready for it?" She tries to hold him in suspense. She is practically vibrating. "It's giant hogweed!" This, apparently, is the funniest thing she's ever heard. Her laughter flattens her. She and the rabbit roll around the floor, entwined, hysterical.

His girlfriend turns her face into his stomach. He strokes her hair.

"You two," he says. "The two of you."

Just as the girl said, met with water, the rabbit doll has come apart.

He enters the kitchen through the mudroom, stomping his boots clean. The rabbit is laid out on the table. All its pieces are where they should be, but deflated. It leaks a thick, resinous liquid. The white fur on its ears—authentic rabbit, peeled from a real rabbit's skull—is orange-yellow and rippling. At the edge of one, a seam is coming undone. A thin wire pokes through.

His girlfriend, still in her nursing whites, is standing at the stove. She looks over her shoulder and smiles.

He asks, "What happened?" Her behavior surprises him. He would expect her to be distraught. This is, after all, a loss. For the girl—a loss.

His girlfriend closes her arms around him, biting a kiss into his neck. "Rabbit—" she says breezily, "got mixed into the wash."

"On accident?"

She's returned to the stove, where something is beginning to burn to the bottom of the pan. "Yeah." A curl of smoke unwinds upward. She clicks the switch for the hood fan. With a wooden spoon, she scrapes.

"Please," he says, "don't lie to me."

"I'm not."

She is. The rabbit is two feet tall and stinks a room away. It cannot be misplaced. He crosses his arms. Exhaustion is a sudden ten-pound weight hung from the bottom of his spine. He'd like to sit, but doesn't.

His girlfriend keeps her back to him. "She's too big for a doll."

"She's barely ten." Why, he asks himself, even start this?

His girlfriend's back is stiff, "So?" She lifts the pan off the burner and dumps whatever it was into the garbage can. "She doesn't need a doll."

He finds the girl in the backyard building something monolithic and red from the snow. Beside her is a box of food coloring. She's mitten-less and without a coat, her shirtsleeves rolled, her hands stained red.

He calls to her, "You."

She abandons the snow she's patting. Close, he sees her eyes are pink and swollen, but her voice is a chirp. "Do you like it? Do you like it?" She points at what can't be missed.

He walks around her sculpture making appreciative noises. The girl is a keen little animal. It takes him perhaps a full minute, during which she becomes less animated, to realize what he's looking at is *them*, a child's family portrait shaped from snow. He takes in the larger snowwoman's massive breasts and unkind stick mouth. An unflattering attempt has been made with food coloring to dress it in something short and red.

Immediately, the girl knows he's solved the riddle. "I made it for my mother." Her small, cold fingers interlace with his. "Should I go get her? Should we show her?"

He understands then, that all throughout construction, the girl assumed his loyalty.

He corrects her, by loosing his hand from hers and taking a shovel to her work. She stands nearby, silent while he hacks away scattering cuts of sculpture across the yard. When he breaks a sweat he stops. In the girl's eyes is something implacable. He plants the shovel in the snow. He rolls her sleeves up past the elbow, then he sends her to the shed to rub turpentine on her red stained skin.

In the kitchen, the rabbit has been cleared from the table. His girlfriend perches in its place. Her white-blonde hair is down. Through it, she watches him, the most beautiful thing he's ever seen, and he wants her, always, to stay that: beautiful and his.

With difficulty, he says, "I need you to try harder."

His girlfriend's mouth opens.

"No," he says, "I mean it."

She does not respond, but holds out her arms, head bent. He steps into them, kisses the part of her hair. She rolls her face against his chest. "I hate it," she whispers, wetting his skin through his shirt with the press of her open mouth, "when you're mad."

He says, "I don't like it when you're mad either. I don't like the things you do."

She says, "We can make it better."

He says, "I want us to be better."

She says, "We can be better."

He says, "That's all I want."

On the first day that volunteer searchers are requested, he and his girlfriend drive out to the fairground that is serving as a base of operations He gets up early to brew coffee. She spends an hour in the bathroom. A door between them makes him queasy. Periodically, he leaves the table, where their coffee mugs are full and waiting, to stand outside the bathroom with a hand raised. He doesn't ever knock. She emerges made-up, her hair in brittle curls, lashes blackened with mascara. He's become used to them white. She moves around the kitchen, touching things. Teakettle. Trivet. Wooden spoon. He sneaks glances. The coffee has gone cold.

They've been advised against participation—a lawyer, himself an enthusiastic volunteer of services, warned, "Don't do it."

See, if they are an active part of the search, if they should find her _____ (here the lawyer leaves an interpretable hole, whose plug could be either *body* or *dead*) then it will look as if they knew, as if they knew where to look, as if they knew what happened, which in turn would suggest, well, it would suggest, it would suggest… (and here the lawyer trails off for a moment, reaching up to smooth the thin hair, spiraled neat as soft-serve around his shiny scalp), but still he recommends that they go, go out to the fairgrounds where the volunteers are gathering, and that his girlfriend, that she, she, she as the mother, she at least, should say a few words, give her thanks—and maybe lead a group prayer?

When they arrive at the fairground, the parking lots are full. The gates are guarded by a boy in an orange safety vest. They stop. He slouches over to their rolled down window. "Full up," he says. "Park it in the plowed field. Anywhere." He points with both hands in the direction they've come from. He's wearing a man's pair of rawhide work gloves, his own small hands lost inside. The gloves begin to slip. The boy claps his wrists together to keep them on. He blushes. "They're my dad's."

In the exhibition hall, giant, round bulbs caged in wire make bars of shadow on everything below. The stadium seats are empty, but he feels gladiatorial. The air holds the same charge that crackles through the aisles of the grocery when a blizzard is bearing down and stock has dwindled on the shelves. An area of the sand has been designated for them. A literal line dug into it. A metal folding chair, seat webbed with frost, is delivered for his girlfriend. From a short distance, a dozen women in quilted vests watch them baldly.

An organizer with a bullhorn calls for attention. The volunteers break into tribes of hope and goodwill. He stands with her, their backs against the curved rail that separates the first row of seats from the ring. A man, who self-identifies as an expert, demonstrates how to stab the snow, using, in his instruction, the words resistance and yield interchangeably. "You're feeling for yield." He watches the man lower himself down to the hard sand and play dead for teenage boys who push ski poles against his chest. "Feel that? Hit resistance, flag it." Still supine, the man continues to give instruction.

His hand is inside his girlfriend's coat, slipped under her shirt to rest on her back. She's sweating. She starts to tell a story, about coming to the fairgrounds with the girl, a few years ago—when everything was horses, horses, horses: that girl-kid phase—to see a trick pony show. The grand finale: a Clydesdale and a little pony are led out on the sand. They're the same color, gray with a white blaze, and styled the same, long manes braided and combed out, with red ribbon bridles. Twins, see? So it gets a laugh, when they bring out one, then the other. The trick starts with the horses walking. The Clydesdale tromps, the pony is doing double time, one going clockwise the other counterclockwise, the pony on the outside, closer to the rail. In the center of the ring their trainer gives some sign, makes a noise, and they start to trot. They go faster and faster until they're running. They're galloping. There are moments when each seems lifted from the ground. Then they're supposed to do something. She makes an **x** with her hands. Cross. A halation—she doesn't know that word, but that's how he pictures it—the sand lit with mica, rising from the bottom of the ring. The horses are supposed to cross, but instead they collide. The pony goes flying. He takes her wrists. Her fingers dig at the base of her own throat. She's sobbing, "Take care of me."

Afterward, the lawyer tells them they've done well. Already, the volunteer effort is scaling back, the staging area moved from the exhibition hall to the smaller ladies' changing rooms. All things considered, the lawyer says, they will not be expected again. "We'll say," he says, his fingers curving into claws that represent quotation marks, "that it's too hard."

Time is a color-shifting jelly. They move through it slowly, achieving new positions in which they stay suspended until another change is forced. He answers certain knocks at the door and certain phone calls. He addresses what he can address, and then breaststrokes his way back to her. In the bedroom, the blinds are drawn and outside it's light or it's dark; in either condition she is a spill across the sheets.

They doze and they fuck, and in between stay knotted, waiting for an urge to direct them. Light arrows through the blinds. It stripes first the floor, then the wall, then the ceiling, and then it goes away—but comes back, again and again. One day is followed by the next. Time passes.

The streetlight's dense electric hum brings him to near awareness. He spends the black syrup of a night touching the lines on the palms of her hands. Outside, snow is still falling, clumped like confetti, interrupting the light from the streetlamp in odd fluttering holes. He lifts his hand away from her, meaning to get up, to adjust the blinds. Sitting, he swings his feet to the floor. His body is enormous and crude. He nearly pitches over the edge of the bed. His fingertips are singing. She lays a cold hand on his shoulder, the other working in his lap, "Come closer. You're too far away now." She falls flat-backed, legs dropping open, and guides him into her. Her heels come up, digging into his buttocks and urging him on, on, on. Against white sheets, she is as white as a funeral bouquet. She touches his face, "Don't cry."

He folds himself around her, rhythm lost, his nose to her temple. "You can cry." Her skin is cold, but her smell is warm, bready and mammalian.

His girlfriend is a slip of paper and he's the envelope she's folded into. His thighs over her thighs, his arms across her chest, her hands closed inside his. With the soft pads of her thumbs she rubs the nails of his pinky fingers. It makes a sound he can feel in his teeth—tiny and terrible. In the bed, their smell has been developing, ripening, growing fat and wet-fleshed under a hard rind. The light from the streetlamp passes in muzzy bands through slits between the blinds. Where it touches their skin, they are turned yellow. She is cold against him, but so wet with sweat she could be melting. The blankets are on the floor. The sheets are sticky, are stiff, are sour. A membrane of filth makes her skin tacky to the touch. More than anything, he wants to bathe her. To tilt back her head, a hand on her brow to protect her eyes, while he sluices cup after cup of warm water through her hair.

It occurs to him that this is the deep end of love, where options are limited. Here, he understands, one treads water or drowns.

Downstairs, alone, he sits naked in the cold. On the television screen, filmed from above, searchers are crows in a field of snow. Then the perspective changes—a return to earth. An officer cups a gloved hand around his mouth, shouting instructions. His breath rises in white wisps, wreathing his head. The searchers, lined shoulder to shoulder, extend their arms, shuffling until an arm's length separates them from their neighbor on either side. They start forward. So emphatic, is that first step, he can see what they believe: Nothing will escape them. Today will be the day.

He goes to the set, clicks it off. Upstairs, his girlfriend is alone in bed. He can close his eyes and see her. He can close his eyes and see through the plaster, the beams, the boards. Above him, she is curled on her side, her cheek on the bony pillow of her folded hands. His eyes closed too long, he can see straight through to her bones. Bones and snow and long white-blonde hair and joyless giant white lilies—a farrago of white things stirring together in the bowl of his skull. His head aches. He rests it against the cold glass of the screen. Today might be the day.

It isn't.

Merrily, merrily—life is but a dream.

It cannot be otherwise, because one day the girl did not come home and when he voiced his concern—a little child, two hours late—his girlfriend shook down her white hair and wound her warm hands, worn from endless washing, into his clothes then whispered against his neck, "Worry about me instead."

Sweethearts

Over the radio, it was announced that a young couple in Austin, Texas have given the name Trout Fishing in America to their first-born son. He will be the second child known to carry that burden, though the first assumed the mantle by choice, legally changing his name from Todd, in October of 1985.

The assumed date of Richard Brautigan's death is September 14th, 1984. His body was not found until October 25th, 1984. I was born on January 1st, 1979. My boyfriend, the only one I've ever had, eventually my husband, was born on the 27th of August one year later. High school sweethearts, people are always asking for the story of how we met.

The town of my childhood had two elementary schools, both clapboard, both quaint, one with gingerbread trim, one without, and which of those a boy or girl attended depended on where that child lived, and where any child lived was determined by the kind of money his or her parents were making.

So—there was no problem there, not for the earlier years, in keeping like with like, but come junior high all children were bussed to one brick building, and certain lines, previously marked, became uncertain and in need of being re-drawn.

Tracking began in the sixth grade—Honors Prep, Prep, or Remedial—and which track a boy or girl completed determined which courses he or she would take when entering high school: Honors, Prep, or Technical Ed. Based on high school courses, students then applied to private colleges, or to the various branches of the state university, or signed up for the service, or took hourly-wage jobs: changing oil, ringing up groceries, gutting rabbits, and began impregnating or giving birth, whichever their gender allowed.

The High School Honors courses were capped at twelve seats to a class, and the children in those seats were all the product of the local well-enough-to-do.

I was the exception.

In my house we had a phone, and its bill must have been the one that was regularly paid, because every afternoon at four my mother unplugged it, so my father, coming home from work, bringing with him a cold smell of butchering and a cloud of loose white fur, would not intercept any calls from the creditors who owned our lives and were owed all of our future earnings.

Is that enough?—these details that I've allowed, or should I lay it out further and more plainly? My family's reputation was questionable with cause, and the life we mutually led was a shitty one.

About the town: there wasn't a factory, but there was a small naval base threatened with closure, a rabbit farm with an adjoining slaughterhouse and packing plant, and a distribution center from which gourmet local foods—chocolate enrobed cranberries, smoked mussels, handpicked crab, and the fresh hindquarters of pink-eyed, snowy-coated, eight-week-old New Zealand Whites—traveled around the world.

In the sixth grade I was put into Remedial Track with the other boys and girls from the intersecting country roads between the distribution center and the rabbit farm. Our houses were shiplap and tarpaper and corrugated tin. In winter we shivered around the woodstove and in summer slept with the doors open and citronella candles in every room. The boys, neighbors through the woods or across the salt marsh, already held the low man's justified suspicion that all direction contained condescension. Some would not continue on to high school, landing in juvenile detention, or the old Quaker graveyard. Some would drop out after their sophomore year, when they would be sixteen, and legally employable at forty hours a week.

They spent our classes playing quarters: a blood sport. One boy would fold his fingers against his palm, hand on the desktop, knuckles out, then another would use his thumb to flick a quarter—and later, heavy washers, notched for damage—sending it across the desk into the first boy's knuckles. The goal was to draw blood. If skin was broken the flicker got another turn, if not, he put his knuckles down.

The class was mostly boys. There were two other girls, who sat together at the front of the room, painting one another's nails with Wite-Out. The teacher had had it long before we got to her.

I spent class in the farthest corner of the room, quiet, with my own book in my lap, until the day the teacher, explosive in the way of ground-down women, charged up the aisle and discovered I was reading Jean Auel.

She opened and closed her mouth. Her face was red. She said, "That book is full of *sex*."

I said, "Yes, ma'am," because it was.

She said, "That's very *adult*."

It did not seem overtly so to me. "Ma'am," I said, unsure.

Later in the day my teacher met with the teacher who taught Honors Track, and I was moved. We read *To Kill a Mockingbird* and I cried for them—the mockingbirds, for Boo, and for Tom Robinson, and for Jem's arm too, broken and forever bent—for the loss of things reasonably desired and unfairly denied.

Three years later, when I was fourteen and a freshman in high school, the Honors English Teacher was a famous man. There were two things. The first was his tall, beautiful wife. She was not local, an import from Arizona or New Mexico, somewhere far away and different. Mysterious and gaudy, she wore a fedora with a velvet band and her arms were circled from wrist to elbow with silver jewelry. I thought she was ridiculous, shameless—always drawing attention to herself—and if I could have looked like anyone in the world, done a body swap, I would have chosen her hands down.

The second thing the teacher was famous for: he was supposed to keep a row of joints, a box of matches and a roach clip in the top drawer of his desk. That he kept the drawer locked—it was tested every time he left the room—was treated as certain proof.

I never did believe it though. It wasn't that drugs were taboo, but rather that they were so common. Whose father didn't smoke a joint in his truck as soon as his shift was over? Whose father didn't come home, untuck his shirt, unzip his fly, roll a joint and smoke, warming his bare feet on the sleeping dog's belly? It seemed an unfitting habit for a man who read so many books. Then, one time it happened that the teacher hugged me, brought me up against him, his arms around me for a slow sigh of time, and with my body so close to his, I recognized the heavy green pungency held in the wool of his sweater.

And life is full of all types of disappointments, but some, are harder.

Something that may help in understanding this story: I was the volunteer. The first time the teacher asked for help, I raised my hand, and I raised it every time after. I raised my hand until the teacher stopped asking for volunteers. He did not have to ask, because he knew he had me.

Alone together, the two of us. Teacher and student. Hours in the storage closet. We had to crack each book and shake it by the covers to check the glue in its spine. How badly were the pages falling out? Every book. We had to check. There was one window, a tiny box of shivering rain-colored light. We didn't have to whisper, but it felt like we did, so we did. And sometimes, as we made repairs, me holding a page in place as he smoothed a line of tape with his thumbs, our knuckles touched.

Hours and hours.

Picture it: this quiet gray work. Air full of dust and sweet mustiness. A young girl, an older man. What a scene is being set.

Would anyone believe me if I said I didn't know?

On the bottom shelf of the book closet, beside two stacks of *Ordeal by Hunger* were three copies of *In Watermelon Sugar*, the one with a blue cover with Brautigan and the smooth-haired girl—and it's all in their eyes, isn't it?—standing one in front of the other, staring out like they're seeing, as if their photographed eyes actually functioned on paper, and under their picture the words: *In watermelon sugar the deeds were done and done again as my life is done in watermelon sugar.*

The teacher held the books to his chest, arms folded over them, his eyes closed, rocking back on his heels.

When he opened his eyes, he said a word that was mostly sigh, then held the books out to me. "You should have this," he said. "You should have these. You take two and I'll take one." He put two books into my hands and then put his own hand on the cover of the top book he'd given me, the third still held to his chest. "I could never teach this," he said. "Not that they would let me, but I could never teach this. There isn't rhyme or reason to it. There just is. It's like—" He pushed his bangs, which were too long, off his forehead and he looked right at me—just a space between blinks, then he blinked, and I blinked, and it was over.

"What?" I asked, because he hadn't finished. "What?"

He laughed. "I've gone and forgot," and he turned away.

An essential detail: the teacher, my teacher, he had two sons with his beautiful wife. One was named Casey. I never knew the other's name. But he doesn't matter anyway.

It was the same year, when I was fourteen, a freshman in high school, that a terrible crime was committed in Florida. The body of a child—four years old was the guess—a little girl, was hooked by a fisherman, dragged up through the brown water of a backyard canal then set on a tarp under a spotlight. The girl hadn't drowned, or been pulled in by an alligator, or been wading under her mother's watchful eye when a jet ski came out of nowhere and flattened her dead. Somebody pitched her, a naked little body, already stripped of life, weighed down by cans of stewed tomatoes duct-taped to her arms and legs.

It was all over the news. She had her own theme music. Every channel was doctors being interviewed, explaining aspiration, and later on, when divers found the Marlins mini bat, rectal prolapse. Aspiration though, was how she died—suffocated while vomiting. When a person swallows water the wrong way, it gets pulled into their lungs, then they cough and it's cleared. She couldn't clear her throat. It was clogged with hair. Her intestines were full of it. Starving to death, she'd been eating it as it fell out.

There were models and diagrams, and everywhere, pictures of the body bag, sagging in the middle as it was carried up a bright green rise, palm trees and the shine of water in the background.

It made it hard to eat. It made it hard to comb hair. It made it hard to swim, to sit out in the sun, to have a crush, to keep a secret, to masturbate, to live at all.

Cleveland, Ohio, is the central hub of the child sex trade in America—the authorities said so. There were nightly news specials about the things that happen to very young girls at truck stops. But there was no outraged, no grieving family, only, as days passed and passed and passed, footage, more footage, new exclusive footage of the girl's funeral. It was played over and over and over again. Her little white coffin, bought with donations, carried by hulking, hunky, weeping policeman to its little dark hole in the ground. It was shown from every side, from every possible perspective.

She was all anybody could talk about and all anybody would talk about. Details were forever being released. Her left wrist was broken, she'd never seen a dentist, her ears were severely infected, she was severely underweight. Everywhere, in every room, on the street, in the supermarket, in the drugstore, in line at the ATM—people gasped and said, "How? How could anyone do it?" They loved the feel of that word—*how*—in their mouths. It was all anyone could say, "How could anyone do that to a child?"

How could anyone do it? What does *how* matter when it's done? *How*, it seemed, should be the very last concern.

But I thought about it all the time.

I may have told my teacher how I felt. He may have nodded. He may have said, "You really see the world."

Or it could be that he told me those things, and I thought, *Yes, really he sees the world*, and then I repeated his words until they became my own and our positions were reversed.

Or it may be that I wanted something like that to happen so badly that after so much hope and time, I've come to believe it did.

I was with my teacher in his classroom, helping check in copies of *Titus Andronicus*. The books weren't from my class. It was something he'd done with his seniors. I read the numbers penciled on the inside of each cover and he copied them down.

It was winter. They'd let us out for Christmas Break the day before. My teacher's classroom was on the second floor and just outside the window, the flag, stiffened by frost, curled slow and snapped. It was quiet enough that we could hear the metal pieces ringing against the metal pole, and I said the numbers quietly, and he said them back to me, nodding on the last number of each sequence. Check, he said, and I said, Double check—and his pencil on paper sounded like a mouse chewing wires inside the walls.

Another teacher came into the room then. He said my name. He dragged his fingers through his hair. This other teacher was dressed in everyday clothes: a chamois shirt open over a Metallica t-shirt and jeans. It was embarrassing for me to see him like that. I knew him as khaki pants and a button-down shirt and a tie. He was much younger than I thought. He wasn't so much older than me. He didn't look like a teacher. He looked like a townie, like he should be shivering, sitting on the curb outside the music store trying to bum cigarettes from everyone passing.

My teacher made a motion with his hand. He looped it through the air, a get-on-with-it gesture, and the other teacher said, "It's Casey."

I expected to be dismissed to the hall, but neither of them looked at me. My body felt huge and clumsy. They'd forgotten I was there. I kept waiting for them to notice. I kept waiting for them to be mad.

The other teacher cleared his throat. He said, "There's a problem." He reached out and clapped my teacher hard on the shoulder, one of those man-to-man punch-touches used in place of a hug, but it was too hard, and the world was so quiet the sound—blunt, flesh into flesh—hung there.

The room was very cold. When the school was out, my teacher had told me, the furnace was turned way down low, only enough heat to keep the pipes from freezing and bursting. He cautioned me, the day before, "Dress in something warm."

"Okay," I had said.

"We don't want to have to huddle."

The teacher's son, Casey, had died of a heart attack, a complication of chronic bulimia. He wrestled in college, something I think I'd vaguely known, and his self-inflicted, but accidental death was all tied up with weight classes and national trials, team oaths.

When school started again after winter break, the other teachers were saying there'd been signs. They stood close, mouths to ears, whispering in the hallways. It was always Casey's name I heard. Mine was there too, quietly passed back and forth.

"Do you know who he was with when he found out?"

"No."

"You do."

"*No.*"

"The two of them."

"Alone?"

"Together."

A year later, we were together, alone in the book closet again. The teacher had pulled me out of Trigonometry class, brought me there, and locked the door behind us.

"Trig," he was angry. "Why aren't you in Calculus? You should be in all advanced classes. Don't you want to go to college? Don't you want to be somebody?"

When I reached out to him, he let me take his hands. I squeezed them in mine. He said—a breath, no clear word, then, "Goddamnit." He took his hands back from between my curled fingers. He pushed his long bangs off his forehead, and they fell into his eyes, and I wanted to touch him so badly, but I didn't.

What happened, is what happened.

He did it, and so did I. I could not say then, as I cannot say now, what was wanted or unwanted, where it is that one thing becomes another, only that what is done, is done, and that we were partners in its doing.

Dominoes—all the events of a life lined up, each one hopelessly dependent on another. People struggle with this, with the idea of fate or destiny, whatever it might be called—following the trail of *ifs* back through time unending. See? How each moment hinges on the next? It's ridiculous, but when a butterfly in Africa unfolds its wings a child in Iqaluit slaughters his family as they sleep, and teenagers everywhere question their existence.

Two years after the nameless little girl was hooked and landed, I was a junior in high school. I was sixteen years old and my English teacher was a woman with thin lips and the long, pebble-skinned neck of a turkey. She held a meeting with each student in her class to determine who would be passed on to Honors the following year.

A coincidence: My mother worked for this teacher's husband. He was a doctor. She did his filing part-time. They had dinner together, often. As friends, my mother said, when she and my father fought about it. What was she supposed to do, she asked, say no to her boss?

The turkey-neck teacher, she did not like me. From the moment she set eyes on me and registered my name, she could barely stand the sight of me.

At our meeting, the teacher did not drill me on vocabulary or the plot of *Tess of the d'Urbervilles*. I was moving to sit down, pulling out the chair across from her. She told me I would not be going forward.

She knew I would not make a fuss about it and that my parents would not either. The workings of the world.

There were others, she told me, more qualified, to whom the space should go. I cannot say with certainty that bias made her choice, only that is how it felt to me.

My name was not on the Honors' list. The papers from the Guidance Office showed I would be in Preparatory classes.

But on the first day of school the following year I found I was enrolled in Senior Honors.

My former teacher, gray-haired with over-long bangs, whose helper I had been freshman year, had taken over as the Honors Program Coordinator.

We passed in the hallway. "Hello," I said, "how are you?"

He stopped, stepped close. He said, "I have a book you'd like."

"No," I said. "Thank you. No."

That year, in Senior Honors English, I sat beside the boy who would become my boyfriend. Later in that same year, the two of us, driving in his car with the radio on. The day after Christmas and it was snowing, everything softened, gray and green. The music faded out into a DJ reading a weather report, and so I spun the dial and watched the orange plastic marker climb the frequencies until it rested on a song just as the name *Richard Brautigan* was sung.

My boyfriend turned in his seat, asked, "Who the fuck is Richard Brautigan?" He had one hand on the wheel and the other hand on the radio dial, and the car jumped the road and plunged, coming, finally to rest, wedged between two pines.

Tassels of nettles and broken glass and snow and blood, chickadees singing *chicka dee dee dee* in the branches above us, and my boyfriend's face, his lips pushed flat, his wet-slow breath. His front teeth were broken, snapped off up near the gumline.

Looking at the mess of his mouth I could not speak or move. I watched him lift a hand, fingers curling toward his lips, watched them straighten and tremble, held just above what was destroyed, not touching. I watched the blood run down his chin following the curve of his throat. I watched his eyes widen and his hand lower, and I watched him reach for something between us, a pale square. I watched him bring it to his burst-open lips, as if to fit into his broken mouth and I moved then and I spoke—I clawed at his fingers. I was screaming, "That's glass! That's not a tooth! That's glass! That's glass!"

"And she saved my life," my husband says.

"Not really," I say.

"She did," he says significantly and everyone is meant to understand he does not mean the wreck, but much, much more. The wreck is only how we got there.

We're famous for it: the couple with that great car-wreck story.

After the punch line—such as it is—someone always asks, "But who's Richard Brautigan?"

Then the person who decides to answer will begin, and whoever they are, what they say is always the same, in that it's always wrong. They say, *The deeds of my life*, or, *Again and again is my life done*, or *The deeds were done as my life is done and as I am done*—

They never get it right. We never get it right. Not even when it's one of us, not even if it's me telling it, is it ever right.

Milk

Again—or still—mother is sleeping. Bedroom blackened against the day, curtains pulled tight, she sleeps and sleeps so the children play quietly; quietly, they play at cards and cat's cradle, quiet sitting-down games where their bodies are almost mostly still, like their mother, again—or still—is sleeping, mostly still.

"Can't I?" the girl, on her knees, is sliding slowly toward the door.

"Don't," the boy is boss, older, bigger, brother.

Eventually mother will wake and like a princess from the movies he feels proud to say he has outgrown—girl stuff, baby stuff—she will turn, she will stretch, the mattress springs will shift, and she will—*Ta-dah!*—emerge. For now though, they must be patient and because he is the boy, boss, older, bigger, brother, he will show the girl how to wait.

"Good," he says when she sits flat again picking up her cards.

How long though, should the children wait, silent and mostly almost still while their bodies are bursting to jump and holler, to roughhouse and ride imaginary horses at full gallop through every room, and most of all, most of all, most-est of anything, of all things, to hang from their mother's arms—how long?

Is it an illness that keeps mother closed up behind the door in a room with curtains closed, the sun shut out, the children shut out, turning slowly, dreaming maybe, but mostly still?

Just sadness—that might be the answer.

Knowledge of the cause of mother's long, still sleep eludes the children, but it's what they know: mother with the curtains closed, the sun shut out, them shut out, mother closed up behind her door day and night, their goodness measured by their own stillness, their own quiet, their own ability to sustain and entertain their own selves, protecting the dream or un-dream that possesses mother and keeps her mostly still.

Life has been this way as long as they have known and though they sometimes question it—Why does she sleep? When will she wake?—it is familiar, more safe than it is scary, though the milk sometimes upsets the girl, as the glasses, measured out, run low.

Milk: while the children sleep at night, before the stillness settles over her—need demanding that she pull the blinds and close the door—the mother readies for her long almost stillness by measuring out glasses of milk, bowls of cereal wrapped drum-tight in plastic wrap, and teaspoons of pressed brown sugar; her children will not spill from the heavy gallon jug they are still too small to pour from, and they will not go hungry, and so, preparations made, she can sleep and sleep and sleep until the stillness lifts.

"Now," the girl counts, little body lit in the open refrigerator door, little fingertip touching each cold glass, "there are three milk left. Once," she looks to the boy, "there were more."

Pleading: P-L-E-A-D-I-N-G is a spelling word on the list in the boy's backpack and that is what his sister's expression is.

"Quit it," the boy says. "Right now," and he draws an imaginary zipper over his mouth, sealing his lips because he can be quiet but still boss—older, bigger, brother. "Shhh." Their mother is sleeping and they must not wake her. Ultimately, she will turn, she will stretch, the mattress springs will shift, and she will—*Ta-dah!*—emerge, but now, now she is sleeping, and they must be patient, silent and mostly almost still.

Victory at cards goes again to the boy, though he meant with all his heart to let his sister win, but she is too little to be very good at anything, even Crazy Eights, even Old Maid, even Go Fish, so it is time now for something else, something quiet and almost still: coloring—a picture for mother when she wakes.

X X X X X the girl writes: hug, hug, hug, hug, hug on a piece of paper she slides under the gap below the door while her brother is occupied with making dinner, the slow pouring of milk from glass to bowl.

Yet, mother still sleeps and the girl wonders, should it have been *O*s, kisses like the princes give to wake the princesses who're trapped in sleep, like Snow White who bit the poisoned apple, because she was kind—*kindness*: the chicken puppets at school teach them about kindness, telling about not being very nice, telling how they pecked the littlest chick because it was littler, and afterward, the teacher, hands in her lap, the puppets back in the chest that stays up on the high shelf, asked, "What was the moral?"—and if her mother is like that, trapped, it should have been *O*s.

Zzzzz—with their hard zig and zag, the boy writes in the letters for the girl on the new picture she has made: mother, sleeping.

Glass

Call it a mystery of my dime-thin heart—this fantasy that has nothing to do with sexual tenderness, or the elevation of my person, physical, metaphysical, or otherwise. What I *want* is to see the Full Moon Glass Shop burn.

Here's what they do in this fine little neighborhood where I'm living as a garden-shed renter, surrounded by mock Tudor mansions, a hundred years gentrified. The Full Moon Glass Shop teaches.

It happens in the back. Classes offered out of sight. Stippling, stumping, flashing, and fusing—whatever those things might be.

At the front, through bell-strung double doors, the Full Moon is an art gallery and jeweler, without—and I'm only being honest—anything resembling art or jewels. Curio cases, and bookshelves, and tables draped with velvet runners display earrings, and keychains, and other assorted school-art-fair-type junk, all of it crafted from streaky glass. Hung from the walls are would-be bowls with lettuce-ruffled rims and propped on the shelves are panes of framed stained glass, meant to be placed into a pre-existing window, to throw colored light through the pieced-together image of what might be an angel, or a fish. At the Full Moon these aren't such different creatures.

I walk around this place I live like I've been released into a maze. I pass lovely houses choked with mullioned windows and herringbone brick, turn sharply at stone wall corners, and come to dead-ends at wooden fences chewed through by the force of a garden's growth.

There's one house completely surrounded by a hedge of pink bleeding hearts. They've forgotten they're only flowers. There comes a point, though, where under the weight of a thousand of heart-shaped petals the stalks fold over and flowers spill onto the sidewalk. The wind blows them through the streets. It's like magic, something so pink behaving itself so badly.

Someone was lead through a desert by a cloud of dust. When I was small I had a picture Bible. My mother wasn't the type, and I consider it safe to assume my father wasn't either, but I had a grandmother who was an aggressive believer. She'd be disappointed to learn that all I've retained are the pictures and the stories I made up to go with them. Faith of the kind she hoped to instill in me is something I know nothing real about, neither its practice nor its history. I say "Jesus Christ!" when I stub a toe.

I am reminded, though, watching the bleeding hearts turn cartwheels alongside cars, of that simon-says-y dust cloud. *Follow me.* Once, I was threatened with no ice cream for a summer after bringing home a report card with a handwritten note that read: *It's time to listen. Where does she go?*

On the sidewalk in front of the Full Moon students gather. I can hear them from down the street. At the right, or wrong—it's a matter of perception—time of day, I'm practically wading through them.

I slow, motivated by the same ugly fascination that causes passersby to pull up alongside wrecks and offer their assistance even as the firemen are trying to block off the traffic with orange cones. I listen.

One student will lift a hand. "A piece of mine is in the window."
Another will respond, "Oh, that?"
"No," says the first. "The napkin rings."
"Ah."
Ah, the students say to one another. *Ah*, a complete summation of value, but having just breathed that soft condemnation never stops any one of them from pointing to their own *my-hands-did-this* monstrosity and saying, "Well, that's my piece." Arms swing like they're divin-

ing rods and embarrassments are water, pointing out lumped objects through the window.

It's the long-time students who say my favorite thing—who after a series of mine-mine-mine, punch things up with, "*Also* my work."

I am a witness. This is what the idle do; they aren't happy either.

My best friend had her first mental break when she was 22. Later, I learned this is common in girls. They take their first tour 'round-the-bend in their late teens or early 20's, then make frequent trips for the rest of their lives thereafter. When it happened, I didn't realize. I honestly thought she was scheming and was annoyed.

In college she'd studied theater. When she announced plans to major in drama, my mother said, "Well that's perfect, isn't it?" Affectionately, her own mother called her Peter, after the boy who cried wolf.

Like a million other girls she believed in herself and in her dreams. If not Broadway then off-Broadway until Broadway, if not off-Broadway then a sitcom to start, if not a sitcom then a soap opera, if not a soap opera then commercials, if not that then at the very least a dating show, just to get her name out, just to get a foot in the door. But after college, our lives were at this point: In the grocery store, in the town where we grew up and had returned to, when we put our bag of bulk-food almonds on the scale, we typed in the code for peanuts to save ourselves a few bucks.

At night my best friend served plates of eggs in a restaurant that had breakfast 24 hours a day. I interrupted alumni's dinners and marital congress with requests for *a donation of 100 dollars, sir—75 dollars, sir—with just 50 dollars—sir, your 25....* In the mornings we were sad drinking coffee, watching the soap operas our mothers had watched when we were little girls.

My mother, during rape scenes, said, "Turn your head."

Her mother said, "Ceiling eyes," whenever an actress came on screen wearing a silky robe.

My best friend wanted me to feel her heart. "Is it still beating?"

I told her, "Life is not an *episode*. Breakfast isn't an *audition*."

Curled on her side in bed, knees to her chest, she said, "I can't get up. Everything is shaking."

I thought that what she needed was a good shake and told her so.

When she stopped bathing and stayed in bed all day humming into her knuckles, I believed she was imagining herself shipped away to a place with chaise lounges on a sun-splattered balcony, where an attentive staff would deliver fresh berries and bottled water, and at twilight, hand out gold and silver sparklers, encouraging those under their care to run wild across the soft lawn as the sun set.

The thing was, I wanted to go to that place too.

I'm sure it happens, the occasional desperate husband, boyfriend, or lover, having been careless with fidelity, feelings, or his calendaring—he flies into the Full Moon and makes a purchase. They do have location. There isn't anything else nearby but a bakery and a mini-branch of the post office, so I'm sure the Full Moon turns some business that way, off the fruits of human negligence.

But the bulk of their income—I've seen it—are these people so eager to *express*, the students gathered on the sidewalk waiting for their classes, wanting so badly to produce.

And produce they do. Then, when their misshapen creations are cooled to solid, they're spread through the Full Moon's front room, price-tagged like the one-of-kind treasures they're not.

Before my life changed, I spent a year teaching pre-school. Eleven four-year-olds, and three were named Jayden. Every mother, though, had read a different book of baby names, because each shared with me a meaning unique to their child. They had God in common, but that was all. During the first week, this helped me to decide how I would say Jayden versus Jayden versus Jayden, and soon it didn't matter they were in triplicate, because one was named for God's will, another for his breath, and another for his judgment.

Growing up I lived in a house in the woods. My backyard had no end. Rather than a sandbox I played in the foundation of a burned-out house. What was left after fire—abandonment and time—was the smell of October regardless of the season, and a deep square hole with rough red dust spread across its bottom. It'd been a house of bricks.

I was on my knees pushing handprints into the dust then bowing low to blow them away. Beside me something shivered like leaves when they're moved by wind, but the hole was empty, except for me, and the dust.

At the time I was reading *Wuthering Heights*. I didn't go back to the remains of the house, but every night, even in the winter, I kept my bedroom window partway open.

When my best friend died we were not friends anymore. What happens when two people love one another then stop loving one another happened to us: I hated her. Had she been in her right mind, she would have hated me too.

She was in her mother's care—the television on low and tender baby talk and bursts of anger. I was there for lunch. Her mother opened a can of soup, and poured it, cold, into a toddler's sippy cup. She saw my expression before I could school it. "If you think you can do better," she said, "go ahead. Step right up."

When I left I was thinking of that photo of dead Marilyn Monroe, where her face is unrecognizable, bloated, and discolored.

For days it was there every time I blinked.

The hardest thing that you can ask a four-year-old to do is cut a traced pony from its paper. It's the legs, the curves of muscle, and those little kicky wings of hair at the ankles. It's too much to ask, really, but I never did it to be cruel. Expectations should be met like walls. Sometimes you can go up and over, and sometimes you can bust right through, but the rest of the time, which is most of the time, you hit them full-force, head-on.

The first time a leg rips off, there may be tears, but the thing is, there's another sheet of paper, another pony, another chance, and when a leg comes off again, there's still another sheet of paper, another pony, another chance to try. Chances are they'll fail. They'll never get the legs out. It'll just be sheet after sheet into the recycle bin or put through the shredder for confetti, but after the third or fourth time the kids don't cry, and they don't expect it to work.

Some days my class had no project to take home. Some days all we did was try.

The day when we were making leis out of newspaper beads and construction paper flowers there was a volunteer mother in class. She wet her daughter's yarn in her mouth before she fed the beads onto it. While the rest of the children cut rough three-petaled flowers, the mother twisted tissue paper to make the pistils and stamens for hibiscuses. Did her daughter have the best lei?

Yes?

Or no?

I suppose it's a matter of perspective.

My first stepfather was a dentist. With him my mother believed she would finally live in the style that she'd always deserved. Initially, my mother's pleasure was so great, such a delightful novelty, that I devoted myself to loving my stepfather. He did the same; he said he hoped we would be friends, and was ever ready with a non-intrusive, one-armed hug.

It was nice, but I'll be honest again and admit that we, my stepfather and I, in the years following, continued to show affection for one another for the same reason that you wind a wire around a battery in science class—to make it spark. We loved in anticipation of reaction and award. In the beginning my stepfather longed to please my mother. Later, he attempted to maintain her happiness because it made his own life easier, and while I ceased to care about my mother's level of satisfaction, I hoped my stepfather would continue to buy me things.

Post-divorce, there was a new boyfriend, whom my mother called rugged in a syrup voice that suggested rugged was not exactly, or all, that she meant.

He announced one night that he was taking us out. Still coming down from life with the dentist, to me that meant fancy. After I dressed I went to boyfriend for his approval.

Meaning—*Am I presentable?*—I asked, "Is my outfit okay? Do you like it?"

He said, "I like what's under it."

In my second year of teaching I quit before I was fired. There was a parental complaint. The mother of a little boy said, since entering my class, all her son's progress had stopped completely.

What do you become when your best friend of a lifetime stops being your best friend, then dies?

I don't know what *you* become, but for a day *I* was the woman, who meeting an old high school classmate on the street leaned close to whisper, "You know—she never was *quite* right."

I'd like to see it all go up. I don't know how high a fire must burn to melt glass, but I imagine it's Hell hot. The firemen would have to stand across the street with their hoses. The whole sky would bend with heat. In the end there would be nothing left but a lesson.

It's no good.

Try again.

Shoot Out

They pass fields yellow and black with gnarl-stemmed flowers, grown waist-high and leaning, shaped by steady, hot wind. They pass fields of dust, chaotic with bleating goats who stare from between tight strung lines of wire as the car slides by, the slotted, sideways pupils of their golden eyes following the girl into her dreams.

Here, at the edge of sleep, her body loosens and she allows her thighs to drift, first wide then wider, until her knee is touching the boy's as he drives. When he shifts away the sound of their separating sweat-damp skin is as delicate as a first kiss.

Kiss: a sweet pink word the girl holds in her mouth until she dreams—and is awake again, blinking to clear her eyes.

Around her the heat is pressure. She floats, but is pinned, out of sorts. In her head and belly is the slung about, locked in feeling of a carnival ride that challenges gravity, the kind with spinning cages and an operator keeping tally of how many stagger off, sick and doubled-over. The girl touches her throat, her stomach. She swallows to loosen the dry gag of her tongue and blink-by-blink becomes aware.

On the seat beside her the boy's undershirt is a shucking as thin as a snake's outgrown skin. Head tipped, she watches him through lashes. His chest is pale, but his arms are tanned in gradation, darkest at the hands, their color marking southward progress through the rolling of his sleeves higher and higher, until today, when the heat has beat the shirt right off his back.

His hands, sunburned then healed, are draped carelessly on the wheel, their new copper color a contrast to a scattering of scars, bright white, across his knuckles. The girl admires these. Her eyes tilt to her own hands, with coordinating lines—matching scars.

"You're awake," the boy is certain, though focused on the road.

The girl straightens from her slump against the window.

"Keep us straight," the boy instructs, and when she puts a hand on the wheel, he folds across her thighs to reach a duffle bag at her feet. There is the sibilant hiss of a zipper then the soft shuffling of cloth against cloth and he begins dropping things into her lap: a sticky box of raisins, a scratched silver-tone Zippo, a pocket knife with a mother-of-pearl handle, his balled-up plaid shirt, a squirt gun that dribbles wet warmth down her leg.

The road bottlenecks without warning. Now they are closed in by low walls of bone-colored concrete, one in a long line of cars, when before they had been alone for miles upon miles upon miles.

Outside, small, dark men in orange vests and battered hard hats stand in a line, shoveling sand up a hill of sand. Ahead, a man is directing traffic with a stop sign and tiring arm. Behind him the yellow landscape bends. Sand lifts off the hilltop, gold-brown, translucent, and fades into the whitish sky.

The girl's eyes drift from the road, the line of cars, the dull red of brake lights, to the boy's head hanging between her legs as he digs through the duffle. With her free hand she touches his hair, made darker and with a curl put into it by sweat. She rests her fingertips on the nape of his neck, a barely-there touch, canting her hips.

The boy rejects her invitation. "Don't," he says, up-righting. Between two fingers, held deliberately by a corner, is an envelope handled to fuzziness at its slit seam.

She pulls in a breath making her body smaller. "I was only playing."

The boy's eyes flick to the girl's hands, one controlling the car, the other docile, curled in her lap.

"I wasn't," he says and reclaims the wheel.

They sit then, in silence. A pattern establishes: ease forward, still, and wait. Time becomes syrup in the way of sugar-water heated and stirred. The man directing traffic gives up on lifting his sign, letting it drop face down in the verge. In its place, he makes limp gestures that are occasionally misunderstood: the procession lurches when *Stop* is mistaken for *Go*.

On the opposite side of the concrete barriers, men in groups of four are laying tar. Two shovel it from a heaped wheelbarrow and two more tamp the rough piles with a metal tool. The air around them bends with heat. The landscape wavers, a science fiction shimmer, the suggestion of a portal to another place.

Ease forward, still, and wait.

Ease forward, still, and wait.

The girl pinches her nose between thumb and forefinger, "That smell." Chemical, oozing-black. "It's making me sick."

The boy, not missing a beat says back, "*You* make me sick."

Instant: the girl in tears.

Jabbing at her with a playful elbow, the boy tries, "Oh, come on." And when she doesn't brighten, "Take a joke."

The girl works her jaw, trying to chew down her feelings. "Why are you so mean?" A sob springs free. And another, and another, because in tears, she knows she has made herself uneven-red, rumpled and ugly.

The boy adopts new tact, "Shh." He tries baby-talk, "Hush now." He lays his darkly tanned hand over the girl's, running a fingertip along her most prominent scar. "Remember this?"

She scrubs a palm over her wet face. "Yeah." She turns her hand in his, fitting her thumb to a white divot at the center of his palm. "Remember this?"

"Yeah."

Leaning against the confinement of the seatbelt, she shimmies close enough to rest her head on the boy's shoulder. He puts an arm around her. She breathes in the heat coming from his skin. He smells like dough: flour and yeast and salt and water. A comfortable, kitchen smell. Homey. The girl knuckles away tears already drying in a fine, granular crust, and sensing opportunity, asks, "What's in the envelope?"

The boy has tucked it into the vent farthest from her. The paper flutters faintly in the air conditioning's thin breeze. The sound it makes is constant, soft and rasping. Like an itch beyond reach, the girl cannot help but be aware of it.

The boy twists his hand free of hers. He raises his elbow again, not playful, but blunt and bullying, prodding with it until she is detached from his side.

The girl curls back toward the window. Heat drums long fingers on the glass. "Sometimes," she says, "you're mean."

"Sometimes," he says, "you stick your nose in."

Ease forward, still, and wait.

Ease forward, still, and wait.

The girl slips in and out of sleep—sun stunned—watching, then dreaming, then watching again, then dreaming.

She dreams a dream half-imagination, half-memory. She dreams a Ferris Wheel at night, the red and yellow and green and blue round lights, the cage that swings slowly back and forth, the heavy safety bar across her lap that locks them—her and the boy— side-by-side, and the summer heat, the starlight, the golden-powder smell of hay spread over the trampled grass to keep it from turning to slurry, and her own nervous, onion-y sweat, and the boy, beside her, yeast-musky and molasses-sweet, his clothes and skin stuck with threads of burlap from the feed sacks they rode down the giant wooden slide, and tucked between them is a stuffed red devil the boy won for bursting balloons with throwing darts, but then it falls, tumbling hooves over horns, falls and falls, as if from a greater height, toward the earth littered with loud people and plywood booths and hay being tramped into mud, and then, as it falls, instead of the devil's prickling synthetic fur, there is the boy, an **L** of human heat fitted to her same shape, and below, bells are ringing, a celebratory hoot rising, and a carnie is crying, "Winnah! Winnah! We've got ourselves another winnah!"

The girl comes fully awake to find she is alone, the car pulled over on the roadside. The windows are down. A scorched breeze drones like a fly that can't find the openness where glass becomes air. She scrubs a hand across her mouth. It comes away whitened with a broken crust of dried saliva.

Groping, she finds the latch for her seatbelt. The metal is scalding hot. Where the belt straps have pressed her shirt is sweated-through.

She plucks the fabric away from skin, twists until joints, bone-in-socket go *pop*.

The boy is nowhere to be seen. She checks forward, back, left, and right. With the caution of someone who knows to be seen in the action they are performing would be to be caught, she slides across the bench seat. The envelope is not tucked into the farthest vent. It is not on the dash. Or under the driver's side on the floor. The girl tries the glove box next. It springs with a long metallic groan. Reflexively, she looks behind her. No one. Next is the duffle, which she opens slowly, tooth-by-zipper-tooth. The envelope is not there.

Outside, the girl finds the boy holding a crumpled soda can over the top rung of a

wire fence. A piebald goat lips at it. The boy keeps the can just out of reach. "Think it's true?" He lowers his arm incrementally. "That they'll eat anything?"

The girl grabs for the boy, "Don't do that. You might hurt it."

He plants a flat palm against her collarbone. Holding the girl back he lowers the can over the wire. Rising up, doing a shambling dance on hind legs, the goat pulls it from his fingers. It shows rectangular yellow teeth, jaw sliding side-to-side. Awful: the sound, aluminum on calcium.

The girl shoves the boy. He stumbles into the wire, but recovers, turning on her so quickly, one arm snapping back, that she drops, covering her face.

The boy lowers his arm. "Hey." Moving close, he grips the back of the girl's head. "Hey," he pulls painlessly until she looks up. He's grinning. His other hand is still a fist. "Two for flinching." The flat smack of his knuckles—once, twice—turns the side of her neck numb. The hand closed on her hair, opens and pets. His fingers run along her scalp. Once, twice.

"Ow," she says.

He gathers her hair up off her neck, drapes it over one shoulder and touches where he punched. "Come on," he says. "You know that didn't even hurt."

Still crouched down the girl reaches out, curling both hands around the boy's shins. "Might've."

"It didn't though."

Under the boy's hot skin, the bone is pitted. Crawling her fingers up, the girl stops at a wide, rectangular dent. "Bicycle pedal?"

"Bicycle pedal," he confirms.

Higher, on the opposite leg, is a round depression, the size of a nickel. "This one?"

"You don't know?"

Hesitating, "—No."

"Ball peen hammer." He aims a significant look at the girl, "Remember?"

"No." Then, "Yes." She positions her forearm like a blindfold. "You had me close my eyes and cover them, then you hit yourself."

"And I said, 'Where?'"

"And I knew it was your leg." The girl drops her arm. "I couldn't see, but I could feel it." She smiles. "When you're hurt, I feel it too."

"Like twins." The boy takes the girl's wrist, but as he draws her up, there—*there* is the edge of the envelope tucked into the waistband of his jeans, flat against his flat belly, and she grabs for it.

The boy twists away. Their bodies become tangled. His knee catches her in the gut tipping her off balance. The girl throws her hands out to catch herself. "You don't have to play so rough."

"You don't have to stick your nose in."

"You don't have to play so rough though." The girl holds her hand out to be helped up again. "You don't." When the boy doesn't answer she says again, "You don't," but lets him take her hands, tugging, pulling her up then along, back to the car.

Shimmying across tacky vinyl into position behind the wheel, he says, "You complain, but what would you do without me?"

She climbs after him. "Die probably."

He fixes her with an indulgent smile, and brings her hand close, examining the palm. The soft meat under her thumb is scored in the ragged circle of an old burn. He kisses two fingers, touches them to the mark then sets her hand in her lap, reaching across to grope in the space between passenger and door. He finds the tail of the seatbelt, untangles it and buckles it around her. She sucks in, hollowing her waist. He cinches it tighter.

"Without you," the girl says, and dipping, reaches into the duffel at her feet, straightening with the squirt gun, "I'd be a goner for sure."

He reaches for the gun. "Did you open my bag?"

She leans away, "Don't tempt me," the barrel pressed to her temple, "I've got a hair trigger."

"That's not funny."

She squeezes. Water dribbles down her cheek. She topples across his lap. "I'm dead."

"Did you go in my bag? It was zipped."

"I'm dead."

"Did you go in my bag?"

"I'm dead."

The boy shoves, sending the girl's limp weight into the door.

She makes a small noise as if in pain.

"That didn't hurt."

The girl replies with silence, eyes closed.

Eventually—a wheeze and squeal—the motor turns. There is the rattle of gravel kicking up. Hot air pushes through the vents. The same faint flutter: paper rippling on a thin current.

The girl stays dead. Dead, until miles later when vertigo alerts her to a shift in direction, the car's straight line abandoned for an exit peeling off the highway, spiraling down.

Down.

There is a miracle then: reanimation. Popping the seatbelt, the girl lunges, locking arms around the boy's neck, "I'm alive!"

Forcefully, with one hand, he unfolds her embrace, "Buckle up."

The car angles along a curving strip into a basin of sand. Distant mountains close around them in a ring.

The boy points, "Look at that." Running parallel to their lane is a wire fence strung with garbage blown from the highway. The insides of candy wrappers and torn bags of chips spark silver on every strand. When the high clouds drift the sun is bared. The light becomes unbearably white. The girl lifts a hand to shield her eyes.

The clouds creep back. The valley grays. Beyond the line of fencing a tiny town desiccates on the desert floor.

They take the turn hard, spraying a rooster tail of gravel.

Dilapidated houses. Low concrete buildings. Dust and rust. Trailers raised on blocks. A pink motel with an illuminated seashell sign facing the highway, inviting: C-O-M-E I-N-N.

They slide past the skeleton of a building with charred beams still standing, then a row of dirt yards boxed-in with wire.

"There's nothing here," the girl says.

At the edge of an unfenced yard, a half-dozen square-headed terriers rear on short chains pawing the air. *Ferocious* is the word for their sound. A block away the dogs forget them. Quiet, then.

"There's nothing here."

The boy swings the car around a corner onto a dirt road, slowing for a child in roller skates, who is crossing to a gas station, a dollar clutched in one hand. Behind the child, a plywood sheet leans against the building. In black spray paint that dripped before it dried: ALWAYS OPEN.

"Is that a boy or girl?"

"Girl."

"Think?"

"You had that haircut." The boy directs the car after the child, thumping into the uneven station lot, stopping at the pump. "Phone there," he says, "if you wanna." Hips lifting off the seat, he digs into a pocket, offers her change. "Go ahead," he says.

She makes a cup of her hands for him to pour into. "I'll call my mother."

He drops the change a coin at a time. "If you wanna."

"Ma," the girl says. "Ma, listen would you?"

"Are you gonna tell me you're in love?"

Through the station window the girl sees the boy at the register speaking with the clerk, a woman with stark white hair. He slips the envelope from his waistband, unfolding the paper inside. He holds it out to the clerk, drawing back when she reaches to take it.

"You could wish me luck," the girl says.

"You'll need it."

"You could tell me you hope I'll be happy."

Inside, the clerk raises one arm then crosses the other over it making an x—no—an intersection: giving directions.

"Why would I do that?"

"Mama."

Silence. Breath. A dog, far away, barking.

The boy jogs across the concrete toward her. "Here." He drags fingers under her nose. "I spilled a little gas so you could sniff."

The girl returns the phone to its cradle. "You're sweet," she says.

The boy rests his slick fingers above her lip. "No shit."

They pass fields of gray-green scrub, muted motel pool colors, black plastic tangled in the branches, whipping in hot, gritty wind. They pass miles of feed lots densely packed with dusty cattle who stare at the passing car, their heavy heads hanging as they wait, day-to-day, to fatten, their sad, fist-sized, jelly-eyes following the girl into dreams.

She dreams a dream half-imagination, half-memory. She dreams a sun-soaked clearing in a forest, soft sand and the sharp, red, dead needles of juniper underfoot, and song birds, small, round, and brown, calling from the tall pines, and the boy is there, crossed-legged in a cradle made by the roots of a giant, rough-barked cedar blown down, and he is flipping open and closed the little bright blade of a pocket knife, and when he says, "I'll shut my eyes," she takes it from him by its skinny mother-of-pearl handle and breathes once then cuts a shallow line across the place where her thumb becomes her hand, asking him, with his eyes closed, both palms pushed against his face—he's blind, sightless, temporarily without eyes at all—"Where does it hurt?"

Then suddenly the road will end, lanes merging into desert, and she is almost awake, and they're closed in by yellow rock, acrobatic cacti dangling from its fissures, and they are lost on the edge of nowhere.

The boy curses; they turn around.

High above, a predatory bird with wings as long as a man's spread arms, dips and soars, buoyed on a current of hot air.

Knocked off kilter, a gimmick signpost, prickled with flat metal arrows, shows the distance to Paris, London, Berlin, El Paso, Las Cruces, Tucson…

The girl comes fully awake as the car stops. They're idling in a dirt yard, a small concrete-block house in front of them. It sits alone with a dizzying beige emptiness behind it. Red chickens scratch in the dirt, undisturbed when the boy steps out into their flock. The girl stays. The engine is running. The air conditioning pushes a thin breeze. She rolls her window down and hangs her head out like a dog.

When the boy reaches the door, a woman is already there watching from behind the screen. The tiny squares of wire—each limed with a dry red fur of rust and stuck with the soft white fibers of some distant flower gone to seed and scattered on the wind—make her appear ethereally fringed.

"I'm not interested." The woman is expressionless, a hand on the screen, the other hanging at her side.

The boy says, "Don't you know me?" He holds up the envelope. "It's me."

From the shadows inside, a young boy, hip tall, steps into view.

The woman says, "I don't know you." She turns, pushing the child ahead of her into the darkness of the house. "You should go."

The boy stands on the step for a long moment then returns to the car.

The squirt gun is in the girl's hand. She's worked the orange tip from the black plastic barrel. The toy is mistakable for deadly now, and her lap is full of water.

Faintly, he asks, "Did you open my bag?"

"Do you love that lady?"

The boy lays his head against the wheel.

The girl reaches across him to cut the engine.

"Do you think you need that lady?"

He lifts his head. There are tears in his eyes.

The girl touches the wet plastic of the barrel to his temple. "Answer me."

The boy's smile, when it comes, is split open. "No," he says.

Slowly, the girl moves in until her mouth covers his. Their teeth touch like teacups meeting in a toast. She tastes tears and the stale water from the gun.

Easing back, the boy's eyes are bright, but dry, and the girl's are full. She leans across him again to turn the key in the ignition. The car rattles to life. The boy puts it in reverse. "I don't need anybody," he says, "but you."

The girl makes a slow show of aiming the gun out the window. As the house diminishes, fading into the background brown, she lowers it. "Now nobody needs to get hurt."

The boy slips his hand into the girl's, his thumb finding the raised line of a scar. "I'd never let anybody hurt you."

Worse Things

This morning the neighbor's gardeners come earlier than usual and drive the homeless girl off her corner with a leaf blower. Once there was a bus stop there, and though the route has been redirected, the sunshade built to protect waiting commuters was left behind.

Normally the girl stays on the corner, dozing upright like a horse, until late morning when the restaurants and shops on the little downtown strip open. She puts in a day of panhandling, staying until the bars close and the university kids stagger away, then returns to sleep under the sunshade.

Now, rest interrupted, and too early to make her way downtown, she walks the curb on her tiptoes, arms out, testing her balance. I see the neighbor's blinds twitch, someone inside following her progress. When the girl is at the point furthest from his door, the neighbor emerges in gold-rim aviators and a sport coat, silver hair brushed back from his forehead.

After he leaves, nodding to the gardeners—who pause, pulling down their bandanas to smile at him—the police come. This is nothing new. Routine. We live, the neighbor and I, in one of the oldest neighborhoods at the edge of the sprawl of the city. Half the houses here have been remodeled into modest haciendas with tiled drives and themed mosaics on the thick walls that block their backyards from view, but the other half are rental properties, small sagging brick ranches with deep scorched yards, slowly succumbing to time.

The neighbor owns, I rent, and the police are called to our little melting pot often enough that the officer responding doesn't bother to leave his cruiser. The car pulls alongside the girl in the street, the window crawls down, and a disembodied voice demands, "What's going on here?"

"Nothing," is always the girl's opener.

The officer says it back as a question. "Nothing?"

"I'm waiting for a friend." She raises a hand to shield her eyes and looks up and down the quiet street.

"Been waiting long?"

"Awhile."

"Doesn't seem like much of a friend."

Also living in the house next door is a girl, lunar pale, who's come out onto the perfect lawn to watch the exchange. In the hollow between her collar bones is a barbell piercing and, below it in an arch stretching shoulder to shoulder, the word *Dolly* tattooed in black Edwardian script.

For the month before I realized she was something else to him, I was certain the girl was the neighbor's daughter, living at home again, busted up by life. I got a kick out of the idea of them, father and daughter under one roof. I liked to imagine his frustration when her spiked shirts tore his khaki slacks in the wash.

When the neighbor left his house, I used to say, "Goodbye, Dad," waving through the window at his stiff back, until the morning I caught the proprietary slide of his fingers up the girl's inner arm all the way to the piercing in her throat. Since then I say, "Goodbye, *Daddy*."

The policeman leaves. The gardeners gather up the grass clippings and leaf litter, muscle their push mower into the bed of a white truck, and go. The homeless girl returns to the sunshade on the corner, the neighbor girl abandons the lawn for the house, and I do not move from my place at the window, watching the small world outside, waiting for the phone to ring.

I won't lie—when I answered the classified ad that had only PHONE WORK and a number, I expected a sex line in need of operators but hoped for telemarketing or a bill-collection service with standards low enough to hire me.

The man who answered began with a question: "Have you ever dreamed of being an actress and seeing the world?"

Fresh off a bus, I'd spent my first week in Houston with a couple of transients from Oregon who'd come to Texas chasing warmer weather. I drifted with them between hostels and motels living off their good will until they wanted a three-way. When we parted company, I had no money, no guarantee of a place to sleep. Dreams were not a factor when I told the man on the phone, "Yes."

We arranged a place to meet. I set terms: public and well-lit.

He introduced himself as Don, "but call me Donaldo." His small, busy hands fanned glossy tri-fold pamphlets across the tabletop, then pushed them into a stack again.

Through flyers and seminars, he sold kits: *Start a Small Business from Home, Secrets for Small Business Success.* He'd set up in a city, stay until things turned bad, then get while the getting was good. "Look," he said. "I'll give it to you straight: It's not what anybody'd call honest work." What he needed—what I would do—were false testimonials, to push would-be buyers into purchase.

"People," Donaldo said, "want connection."

I'd gone in ready to accept whatever work might be offered, but before I could say so, he held a hand up: *Wait.* He cocked his head toward the coffee shop's front window. Outside, rain was falling, heavy and slow. Through the glass, we watched a barista in a clean black apron shooing a homeless man from the protected space at the top of the stairs. "You might think this is bad," Donaldo said, touching the tri-folds, "but trust me, girl, there are worse things."

At the bottom of the stairs, the homeless man thrust a hand out at passersby rushing through the rain.

Set on a sturdy cardboard box in my new living room are three phones in a neat line. On a strip of masking tape across each there is a name and a dollar amount. Women call and I confirm that, yes, I made ten, fifteen, twenty-five thousand dollars selling handmade candles with my *Start a Home Business* kit.

I'm Mary, or Shelia, or Crystal, a voice that authenticates the existence of an invented woman quoted in one of Donaldo's glossy brochures.

Along the far wall of the front room, kits are stacked, ready to be addressed and sent. At first I only did fake testimonials, but then asked to take over shipping for a pay raise.

"What you do on the phone is fraud," Donaldo warned, "but putting shit through the mail makes it serious."

"Okay."

"You could get thirty years. Like, in prison. Real shit."

"There are worse things."

"Christ," he said. "Are you pulling my leg?"

"I want to rent a house. I want some privacy."

We were sitting on the stairs outside the apartment Donaldo had set me up with. Below us, a group of teenagers were wrestling in the small, bean-shaped pool. A girl was shrieking, hands crossed over her chest, a boy jerking at her bikini top.

"What do you need privacy for?"

"I'm sick of living where all the doors all face one another."

"What do you care?"

From the pool there was a "Whoop!" and the boy swung the girl's top above his head.

"I want space away from other people."

Donaldo shook his head. "Jesus Christ."

"It's a win for you."

"I don't know why," Donaldo said, "but I thought you were smarter."

Inside each *Start a Home Business* kit is a five-pound bag of bleached beeswax chips, five bottles of scented oil, plastic pipettes, and string wicks—just add heat. Voila.

I'm white, I'm black, I'm brown. A mother, a daughter, young, old, life-beat beyond age but getting by. I'm a success.

Mary is the one without any fucks left to give. She's older, worked herself paper thin for two kids who both turned out degenerate. Addicts. "They sure as shit didn't get that from me," she says. "They went out looking for it all on their own." The last time her son came around for money, she wouldn't give, so he kicked out the headlights on her car, screaming, "Bitch," until the people across the way called the police, and that was that. "If he was burning," she says, "I wouldn't waste the piss."

Initially, her coldness puts some women off, but if they stay on the line, they'll come to admire her. Mary proudly makes do with very little. "You only need what *you* need," she says, "to be an independent woman."

At first, there were scripts, guidelines for taking calls, but now I improvise.

Readying for the East Coast's eight o'clock, I'm up in early-morning darkness.

I navigate my way into the living room using the bleed of the street-lights through the blinds. I pull their string. The kinked panels clump lopsided halfway up the window. Outside the sky is still blue-black and heavy, Orion's belt bright.

Drie Konings, I learned in school: Three Kings.

"Fuck kings," my sister had said when she learned about the stars' less common name. *Drie Sustres*: Three Sisters. She was at the mirror, torturing her bangs with a curling iron. "Girl power," she raised a fist.

"Yeah," I said.

"*Fuck* yeah," she said.

I mean to shower, comb my wet hair, and dress from top to bottom. Shoes. Bobby pins. The whole works. It's a trick I half believe in—preparing as if there's somewhere I have to be. But this morning I allow the routine to slip. Rather than wash and dress before the phones start ringing, I stand at the window, looking at the city through the line of chewed-up palms, watching the stars' rare shine pushing through the light pollution of a million-plus lives until it's canceled by the new day.

I check for the homeless girl under the sunshade. She isn't there, but the neighbor girl, white as a candle, is standing at the edge of her perfect lawn.

It's serious business to maintain a lawn like that here. The heat and the pollution work against a velvet blanket of green. The city's worst wards are being razed and rebuilt and abandoned and rediscovered, razed and rebuilt again. Here, in our nice neighborhood, we share the same air as there. Air that is made visible by dust and debris.

The neighbors' sprinklers run every night, not just feeding their lawn but washing it clean. For the first week after I moved, I was sleepless from all the strange sounds in the dark. The hiss of the sprinkler heads kicking on would jackknife me out of shallow dreams, heart alive, then I would wander through the little house, peeking out the blinds, afraid I'd find a demented eye staring in.

The first time I saw the neighbor girl, waxy pale, standing on the clipped grass in the middle of the night, she scared a short scream right out of me.

This morning I can see where she's stepped. The water is displaced, leaving dark green tracks. On the concrete too there are prints—hers—the wet curves left by bare feet, leading into the sunshade then back to the lawn.

I go to the front door and unlock the deadbolt. Underfoot, my grass is brittle, sharp, and the air has texture, wet and almost pulpy, humidity rising with the sun. Sweat prickles under my breasts and in the small of my back. "Hey," I call. The neighbor girl turns in her doorway. She's in something small and black with a dozen skinny straps. "Have you seen her?" I point to the sunshade.

She shakes her head and slips inside.

Near the park outside of City Hall, signs prohibit "urban camping" and the consumption of alcohol. Posted too are hours for the use of public spaces, which also go ignored. Mornings, the wide shadowed walkways leading to the park are full of homeless people. Nearby their dogs pant against the swelling heat, eyes half closed but still on guard, lazily alert.

I skirt a fat-headed terrier lying on the sidewalk where the water overflowing from a planter has made a thin puddle on the concrete. It raises its head when I get close, then yawns tremendously, rolling to present its belly.

It's not even seven o'clock, but there is a snarl of men and women at the pick-up counter of the coffee shop. Two teenage girls in pop-bead bracelets with half-shaved heads and greasy backpacks are stealing drinks.

The older of the two is bolder. In the midst of the pre-work rush, she saunters up to where the barista has just set a sweating, clear plastic cup full of coffee over ice. She passes it to the younger girl, who takes a hard pull, her mouth puckering at the bitter taste.

Pushing, the older girl directs the younger to the island of cream and sugar and napkins, then goes back to the counter. "Hey." She raps dirty knuckles on the polished wood. "I'm still waiting on an iced coffee."

Behind her a woman adds, "Me too. The same thing."

I watch the younger girl's eyes go huge. Grimacing through it, she gulps the coffee down; then, red-faced, shoves the cup deep into the trash.

The older girl moves back, slings an arm around the younger one's neck, and pulls her close. "Chill," I hear her whisper. "Just follow my lead."

There is another person who does what I do. A man, named Lix. Volume is one half of the reason for two of us, gender is the other. The home business kits are candle-making: women's work. But who do women trust to make their business a success?

"Not women," Donaldo said, "that's for fucking sure."

Lix gives financial advice for *Small Business Success.*

"Lix?" I asked Donaldo.

"Elixir."

Donaldo lowered his voice. "Former medicine man."

"He was a medicine man?"

"Christ, are you serious? He was a drug dealer. *Elixir.* Get it? He's got the cure for what ails you. Jesus."

When I met Lix, the first thing he said to me was, "You've got a nice voice." He nodded and pumped my hand up and down hard. "Now, can you talk like a black girl?"

We were living in month-to-month rentals across a narrow concrete landing from each other, studio apartments Donaldo paid the deposit on. Sometimes we walked to a little market up the street that had candies flavored with chili and lime and small tabs of hard-shelled violet gum. The register was behind a wall of bulletproof glass. There was a circle of holes bored through, just enough to let the clerk's voice escape. When he rang up my total, I fed dollars through a narrow slot below. Passing back change, not even the clerk's fingertips crossed to my side of the partition.

Lix and I would sit side by side on the landing, each on a call, a plug of tough purple gum in our cheeks, speaking softly, telling happy-ish stories about made-up lives.

The concrete held the day's heat. Traffic was a steady whir. Somewhere nearby, fireworks were lighting off. *Pop. Pop. Pop.* But there wasn't any smoke in the wind, no scraps of thin, singed paper tumbling around, no pleased whoops as the report faded, and I realized it was gunshots.

Lix flashed an imitation of a gang sign. "Gettin' down in Hustle Town."

He would half-listen to me on my calls, shaking his head when I didn't sell.

"Do you know what shameless means?" He shook me by the shoulder. "Baby, it means you got *no shame*." Hooking an arm around my neck, he pulled me against his side. I laid my head on his shoulder. "You watch me. Just follow my lead."

Now when I have a single mother on the hook, admitting she can't make rent and buy the kit both, I'm not above saying, "What about a payment plan?"

Lix taught me that.

I've seen the older of the two girls before, but not in the coffee shop. She panhandles with a sign that says SMILE, and once I saw her standing in the mouth of a walkway late at night, watching sullenly while two men, shirtless, in cargo pants and beanies, negotiated her value. One man handed the leash of his dog, a squat brindle terrier, to the other, then he turned and said to her, "Let's get something straight between us," grabbing at his crotch. I watched the girl follow him into the park.

The tangle of people at the coffee counter begins to thin, and now I watch the girl snag two more drinks, then sling her arm around her younger friend and get while the getting is good.

After they're gone, a woman still waiting for her order realizes that it's been taken. "I can't believe this," she says. "I can't believe this. Those girls were *stealing*."

Behind the counter, a boy in a clean black apron pours cold coffee from a pitcher into a shaker of ice. He will not meet the woman's eyes. "Stealing," she says again, turning in a tight circle, inviting anyone to share in her feeling of violation. "What I'd like to know is where are the parents? Who lets them run wild?"

I'm looking away, but because I'm close she takes a step toward me. "Can you believe this?"

What I could say is, *Yes*. But what I say is nothing at all.

It isn't hard to end up adrift. Take a small-town girl, teenaged and bitter, cursing the small-town stars overhead, believing elsewhere they must be brighter. Make her certain those better stars will guide her more truly. If her roots aren't deep, a strong night breeze will lift her, carry her up-up-and-away, star-ward, then drop her back to earth.

I grew up knowing my mother loved my sister and me, but would always love us a little less than any man who passed her on the street and whistled.

"Don't be jealous," she would say.

The first time my sister was sent to juvenile detention, it was for a boy. After a football game, in the full parking lot, he pointed to a car and told her to break its windshield. She did. The boy helped her dismount the hood. "See how good I've got her trained?" He held her by the back of the neck. "This is my bitch," and she glowed.

My sister became part of the sinewy collection that filled a bestiary run by the state. Released, she found herself caught again, and again, and again.

Our mother would say, "She made her bed. She can lie in it."

We moved to a smaller apartment. I slept on the couch. In the bedroom, my mother and her boyfriends fucked and fought. They staggered out sweaty, wrapped in sheets. I learned the smell of semen and to differentiate between sounds of an orgasm and sounds of pain.

I found other couches to sleep on.

One year, I did not get a call on my birthday. At Christmas, I did not call. That makes a year without speaking. How easily does a year become two? Two become three? For the Puritans, seven years without contact was good enough to call a person dead.

I'm Shelia, soft-spoken, still tender with shame, admitting into the phone, "There were some real bad times—you know?" The woman on the line is hooked, but when the police cruiser rolls slowly down the street I drop the phone to chase it.

I flip the deadbolt and throw open the door. The heat bugs are thrumming and the air is stupid hot. Underfoot, the grass is dead, hard and needle sharp. I wave my hands above my head to catch the officer's attention. Braless, my breasts are everywhere. Early afternoon and I'm still wearing the T-shirt I slept in.

The cruiser bumps to a stop, one wheel on the curb.

I cross the lawn fast, like every step doesn't hurt.

The window lowers. "Ma'am?"

I recognize the voice. *Been waiting long?* "There's a girl," I say, "who sleeps here," pointing to the empty sunshade on the corner.

"She hasn't been here for three days."

"If she comes back—"

"I'm not complaining—"

"Ma'am?"

"—I'm concerned."

The officer fishes a washcloth from his pocket. He uses it to dab sweat from the clean edge his crewcut makes across his forehead. "Ma'am."

I don't doubt that my T-shirt is see-through. Sweat is gathering in the small of my back, running down my ass. I wrap an arm across my breasts and drop the other to cover my crotch with a splayed hand. "Please don't ma'am me."

"Ma'am," the officer says, "Don't you figure she's just got somewhere else to go?"

"No."

"Look—"

I look at him.

He looks back.

"Never mind," I say, turning toward the house. Every step hurts, and I move slow.

I've left my door wide open. The neighbor girl's is open too. She stands half-in, half-out, watching, still in a black slip, a black sleep mask stitched with little cat ears pushed up on her forehead. She lifts her hand in a half-wave.

Closing the door turns the heat bugs' volume down to a background sizzle, like eggs cracked into a pan of boiling grease. Under it I can hear a tiny voice calling out, "Hello? Hello?" The woman is still on the line. "Is anyone there? Hello?"

There's a knock at the door. I set the phone back in its cradle.

The neighbor girl is on the other side holding a carafe of coffee. She's pulled on a pair of loose black pants but is wearing her slip as a shirt. "I just made this," she says. "I just got up too."

In the living room I watch her take in the boxes stacked high against the wall, the row of phones, the absence of furniture. She asks, "You live alone?"

"Just me."

My mind jumps to Donaldo that night on the apartment steps. After he said, "but I thought you were smarter," he grabbed my hands. He brought them to his chest. "I think you're smart." Through his shirt, I could feel his heartbeat kicking up and his skin getting hotter. "Girl," he said, and his nervous little hands were clenching and unclenching around mine, "I think you're a real kick in the pants."

There was no space to retreat on the narrow stairs. "This is how it is?" I grabbed at his crotch, fondling. "You should have said from the start."

"Jesus Christ." He shoved my hands back. "I've never been anything but a friend to you."

The neighbor girl accepts two plastic cups, pouring coffee without comment. She settles herself to the floor. "That's lucky. Just you. I'm married."

"I know."

"Do you want to ask?"

"What?"

"Why I'm married to who I'm married to."

"Do you want to tell me?"

She sips, eyes closing. "It was love." Her mouth pulls down. "He was so nice to me that I fell in love with him."

I sit across from her, brushing dead grass from the sore soles of my feet.

"I bought it hook, line, and sinker." She shrugs. "I'm got. He doesn't have to be that nice anymore."

"I'm sorry."

"It isn't your fault."

"I can still be sorry."

Lix had a sad-sack-of-shit story too.

When he was seventeen he got busted with weed and pills on school property. He mouthed off to the officer, and later he mouthed off to the judge. Juvenile detention, it was decided, until he turned eighteen.

On a school bus with wire over the windows he rode north, past pine forests and dark blue lakes. Crossing a river on a one-lane bridge, he looked down and saw a bull moose as big as a truck licking lichen from the rocks. "Its tongue," he said, "was about as wide as my face."

Juvenile detention was a massive old brick building in the shape of a bird. Only the central tower, the body, was still open. The wings—with windows boarded over and plastic draping all the interior doors—were in the process of being gutted by asbestos removal experts. The township was fighting the historical society for the right to tear the whole thing down.

During the day Lix took classes on woodworking. He built a napkin holder, a birdhouse, a serving tray with beveled handles, then a coffee table, then a writing desk with delicate bowed legs.

At night, fireflies glowed yellow-green in the tall grass. The boys caught them in the industrial-sized peanut butter jars the cook saved for them. There were no fences. Cold air rolled down from the mountains. Wild lupine grew shoulder high with stalks so thick the boys would use them as play swords. Frogs lived in the defunct fountain. After lights out, Lix shimmied into his blankets and fell instantly asleep.

"I never slept so good," he said. We were sitting together on the narrow stairs to our shared landing, knees touching.

"It sounds like summer camp."

"Except there wasn't any swimming there or, like, canoes. But the woodworking, and—" he looked up, a plane droning overhead, "the outdoors part. Nature."

"And bunkbeds."

"Yeah." He grinned. "Bunkbeds."

It was four months and then they sent him home. He wasn't eighteen yet, but he'd been good.

For his first dinner back, his mother made lobster, and mashed potatoes, and corn-on-the-cob.

"I could've ground her throat in," Lix told me. "I could've killed her." The sunset was melting in sherbet colors and his shadow threw itself long. "I could've killed them all." Lix moved to the landing, circling an invisible table, slitting invisible throats with big cross-body jerks of his arm.

All his life he had a sensitive stomach. His father was a dockhand who brought home lobsters that couldn't be sold, and the smell of them made Lix queasy. He would retch and his father would smack him and say, "Not at the table."

It was summer, and the whole family was crowded into the hot kitchen. His mother turned to him and said, "You're at least gonna *try* it." She took a lobster from the platter in the middle of the table. With a twist and a crack, she separated the tail from the body. Fluid sluiced out the tomalley and roe.

Lix vomited on his plate.

"Fucking lobster." He spat on an invisible body. "That's what you get for trying to feed me fucking lobster." Bent, hands on his knees, he was breathing slow and shallow. The pose made him look as if he'd just come out of a fight, but it was impossible to tell if he'd won or lost.

Lix scrubbed a hand over his head, sighed, and sucked in a deep breath. "Some welcome home, right?"

"What's your favorite?" I asked. "If you could have anything?"

Lix straightened up. "Really?"

"Yeah."

"You know what I like?"

"What?"

"Grilled cheese."

Neither of us had a pan, but at the convenience mart we bought Kraft slices, and a long loaf of soft white bread, and heavy aluminum foil. It was behind the counter with the cigarettes and batteries. To buy, I had to show I.D. and sign a form.

"Weird."

"Drugs," Lix said.

Where a car window had been broken out, the street glittered.

Lix squatted down. "Want a piggyback?"

"It won't cut. It's safety glass."

"So?"

He carried me to our apartment complex and up the stairs. My arms were around his neck, my legs around his waist.

When I cut myself on the serrated edge of the foil box, I thought it was funny. "Is this ironic?"

"Bad luck and cheap packaging." Lix put my bleeding finger in his mouth and sucked. He licked the pad. "All better." He grinned, all bright teeth. "Healed with a kiss."

"You have me," I said.

"What?"

"You have me." I caught one of his hands. "To be your family."

He pulled back. "Are you nuts?"

"We're like a family now."

"Jesus," he said. "You're nuts."

I followed him across the room. "I don't mean like boyfriend-girlfriend."

He held up both hands. "Stop."

I used his real name, "Matthew," reaching out.

He crossed his arms, his body going tight. "You need to go."

"No."

"You do." He jerked his head toward the door. "Go."

"Matthew."

"You gotta go."

"Matthew."

He moved fast, grabbing me by the arm and pulling me to the door. "I won't ruin what you've got going, working with Donaldo, but you better stay away from me."

"No." I was crying. "Matthew." He had me half out the door. "I can't believe this," I said. I would have said, "You don't really want me to go."

But he pushed me out. "Believe it," he said.

The sunshade is empty.

From the window, I can see the neighbor girl in her SUV with her little terrier. I watched her carry out two bags and put them in the back, but they've been there, idling, for an hour.

I'm Crystal, promising, "My life has never been better," but I'm thinking of Donaldo and the hurt in his voice, "I've never been anything but a friend to you," he said.

Crystal believes we can all change. "You have to trust that good things can happen."

The woman on the line says, "I want to."

Crystal is the encouraging one. "You can change your life," but I'm thinking of Lix and the anger in his voice. "You're nuts," he said, because I offered him love.

Mail falls through the slot to the floor. I collect it, phone pinched between my chin and shoulder. It's all for former tenants. Nothing comes in my name.

"We all have to live in this world," Crystal says, "but you get to decide how you want to do it."

I flip through a magazine for someone who doesn't live here anymore. A space-filler column called "It's Not All Bad," about a parakeet rescued from a storm drain, is set alongside the feature article. In it, army translators are accused of raping villagers with fluorescent light tubes.

There is video, the article says.

Regimental Reconnaissance Company

Fall—the first day in a week without a drenching rain, and their biology teacher has released them to the out-of-doors, armed with nets and vague instructions. "Catch," their teacher says. "That's *catch*, I said—not *kill*."

Technically, they are teammates, coupled-up in the classroom by counting-off—both are the number seven—but he's abandoned their clipboard and identifying sheets, using the handle of the collecting net to punch holes into the soft ground before bending and spitting. Unaware that she is watching, he calls her over. "Hey, look at this." He points at a hole, his saliva a ladder of bubbles inside. "It something's eggs," he says. "Maybe spiders."

It's late afternoon. A gray dampness is rising. Her dress is seersucker, meant for summer. She is already cold. Moisture prickles along her arms, and she can feel the slight weight of water settling on her hair. She hitches her skirt up anyway and kneels. "Yes," she says, one eye closed, the other an inch above the hole. "I think you're right."

After school, he offers her a ride home. She accepts, even though he's been to juvenile detention, the State Work Farm, twice. Once for smashing mailboxes, again for setting a dumpster on fire. To become a senior, he's repeating the sophomore and junior classes he failed the first go-round.

A soft rain is falling steadily; it's turned meanly cold. The seatbelt on her side does not lock. She holds the strap across her lap. The car fishtails on a corner. She slides into him.

"Black ice," he says, calm.

Rather than home, he drives her to the boat launch. It's abandoned in the off-season, an empty lot. The tide is pulling out. The view is mud. As soon as he cuts the ignition, the windows start to fog. She'd like to go home, but doesn't know how to ask.

He touches her hand. "Are you cold?"

She is, but is afraid that saying so will seem to him some sort of invitation—that he'll say, *Let me warm you up then.* "I can put the heat on," he says, and shrugging loose of it, holds out his coat. "You're all goosebumps."

He shows her how to shear a sheep. "You be the sheep," he says. He's sitting cross-legged and pulls her up into his lap, her back against his chest. The first time he was at the work farm it was shearing season. "I was the newest," he tells her. His hand rests tentatively on her belly. It's warm through her shirt. "There's a gag they pull on the newest guy. They only send the tups his way." She tips her head back against his shoulder, mouths the word, *tups*—the young un-castrated rams. He closes an arm across her chest. "You pinch the rear legs between your calves and thighs, then start clipping." And the tups, he explains, every time—something about the position or the vibration—get a monster hard-on. "Then you're the homo-sheep-fucker 'til they let you go."

She puts her hand over his, each fingertip on a dry knuckle. "But you didn't do that to anyone?"

Through her shirt she can feel his short, square nails, his light touch, like a daddy longlegs haunting across the floor. "It's the only reason to go back," he says.

While his father is away on a hunting trip he invites her to a family dinner—just him and his mother and her. "You're my girl," he says. "You gotta know my ma."

Meeting his mother at the door, she is struck by their similar coloring, their identical noses. In her family there is no one she resembles.

As a hostess gift she brings a bouquet of zinnias. They are beginning to turn, the last flowers of the season. When she holds them out in offering, his mother says, "Well, I don't have a vase." Embarrassment blooms in her belly. But, then his mother goes to the sink and fills a drinking glass with water, turning back to ask, "Is it an aspirin that makes them live longer?"

Some of the petals are already curling under, and the yellow centers are crisp. She does not know the answer. What might make the flowers live any longer? They all look near-gone. She volunteers, "If you hang them upside down for a week then each petal is a seed."

"This place is rented." His mother shrugs. "If we had our own yard, but here I'd be planting them for someone else." She crushes a capsule between two spoons, "Let's give it a whirl," and stirs the powder into the glass. The water around the stems goes cloudy.

At the table, his mother starts a story about him as a little boy—a time they went to the fish hatchery to walk around the outside tanks and have a picnic lunch. There were cost-a-quarter gumball machines full of pellet feed or flakes. Sprinkled, the water boiled silver with fingerling trout. His mother stops, moving away from the table, coming back to serve a second helping of mashed potatoes on top of the first, uneaten portion on her plate. She sees that his mother is nervous, and she asks her, "What happened next?" preparing a little laugh, holding it in her chest for when the story turns funny.

His mother continues, telling how her husband bought a handful of food and divvied it out between them—him, her, and their son, who was still small. Maybe six, his mother guesses, maybe five, and then she shows, demonstrating with an open hand thrust out over the table, how rather than pinch a portion of feed into the water her son opened his little fist and let it all go. She finishes the story, "—and his father was so mad," with her eyes down, hands fraying her napkin.

"Ma," he says, gentle.

"I forgot." His mother looks back and forth between them then stops on her son. "Until I was saying it, I forgot that we didn't have a nice day."

They are sitting in his kitchen, the packets from an MRE spread on the table. He holds up the largest, reading, "Meal, ready-to-eat. Individual." At the recruiting office, they give them out to boys who pass an eligibility questionnaire. Outside the light is shifting. It's getting darker faster now, and earlier, the changing of seasons, real cold weather coming. She can feel it through the gap under the door where the rubber stripping is torn away. When she leaves there will be a glaze of frost over everything. The draft moves around her ankles. She stretches her stocking feet under the table to rest her toes against the bones of his shins.

Thin shadows reach and retract on the wall, the wind blowing the highest branches of the lilac bush across the window glass. She points, flexing her toes, "That could be an elk." His eyes flick up and down again. He's worrying a red envelope of instant coffee between his hands. She thinks of his mother, that night at dinner, tearing up her napkin while she told the story. Tucking her feet under her, she kneels in the chair, leaning over the table. Fingers spread wide, she gives him a rack of horns. He starts to duck away, but pauses to flatten a kiss against her wrist. Miserably, he says, "Everyone I know has a car with a sound system."

"Okay."

"You get like four hundred dollars, just for signing up."

There is a coyote that runs along the tree line at nightfall. She can see its orange body, bright in the declining dusk, slipping through the rows of corn, coming toward the yard. At night, it kills the laying chickens—clumps of feather attached to gristle and wet knobs of bone scattered through the backyard and fields, and in the pea rows there is what looks like dog shit, neatly piled between the indentations left by long rear feet.

A cornrow shivers, then the next, then the next, moving closer. She tells him she has read that coyotes are shy and secretive. "Shy, my ass," he says. He is sitting with her on the back steps, snapping the stems and ends off tough green beans, watching where she points. Once they see the shine of eyes. He plays the coyote, whispering, "Do you see me?" His hands are on her shoulders, then wrapping loose around the back of her neck. "I see you." He tightens his grip. She is a step below him, leaning back against his knees. He flicks a stem into her hair, picks it out. There is a ripple in the tall grass between the corn and yard. He whispers, "I'm watching," and bites down high on her neck, just behind her ear.

It's the first night they spend together. His father is away, hunting again, and his mother has gone up north to see her family, to help them lay straw on their blueberry fields to burn in the spring. Her father is staying with a woman, and her mother is long gone, moved on, and there are no parties, nobody around, nothing else worth doing.

They don't have sex, but she gains an appreciation for what the health teacher always says: *It's best not to lie down.*

The next morning, early, she is awake, and he is sleeping with his face pressed to the pillow. There is frost on the inside of the window. There'll be, she thinks, nothing else from the garden. Through the iced glass, the light turns everything faintly blue. His naked shoulder, the skin pulled thin over the angle of the bone, his dry, deep creased knuckles, the fading summer freckles on his nose and below his eyes—blue. She kneels up, barely moving, light as smoke, careful not to wake him. With the heel of her hand she melts a circle on the glass. Outside it is raining so thick and slow that for a moment she thinks it must be snow.

She dresses quietly, goes to feed the animals. Her rabbit she saves for last. A big white doe, with a black mark in the shape of a heart on one haunch. It lies stretched long in its hutch. Her rabbit is a new mother. There is a whelping box full of pink sealed-eyed kits in the far corner. Opening the door, she shakes what she has brought—bean ends. The rabbit stays splayed, nose working, making no effort to come to her. She holds a piece of green out to it. The rabbit works its mouth, but does not eat.

She thinks it must be something with the kits. She cannot see over the wooden lip of the whelping box, so she reaches her hand past the rabbit to feel inside. Sometimes a doe will eat her litter, or the kits will all freeze, or they are born sick and turn hard as little rocks with their tiny par-formed faces crusted over. But under her hand these feel fine, warm and soft, twisting against one another. It's as she pulls her arm back that she sees the blood on the wire, then the shine of something that belongs spooled inside a body, slick and lavender, stuck to the hutch bottom connecting back to the rabbit's legs. The doe, she suddenly sees, is missing her hind feet, one gnawed off high, dangling long, meaty-strings, the other blunted, without toes.

He is still sleeping, his face to the wall. She had this idea of how it would be to spend the night together, to wake up together. It would be nice to be able to remember it differently, like to remember it with them waking up in one another's arms, pressed close against the cold, the soft light of morning coming through the iced over window. Maybe they would have rolled together and gone back to sleep.

She says four times, "...and chewed its feet off through the wire," before he understands. Her hands are on his chest. He puts his over hers.

With the rabbit draped along the inside of his forearm, its softest skin touching his softest skin, he tells her he learned how to snap a neck in detention, when he was, for the second time, at the State Work Farm. "Lambs," he starts, but stops. He keeps the rabbit close to his body, his hand between its rear legs, cupping over the tail. His other hand is under the chin, fingers curled, his wrist flat between the ears. "It's one sharp pull," he says.

The kits are harder. Together, they go through the options. Fill a bucket and dunk them, throw them to the rooster, or leave them be and they'll die in time. "It'll only take a day," she says. He is shivering. His jacket is in the house. He asks if there is another doe with a litter, and yes, there is, but no—it'll only eat them.

"You pick," he says. "You pick. I'll do it."

She picks.

He upends the whelping box into an empty feed sack and she runs to the barn to turn on and un-coil the hose. The spigot resists turning. The water, coming up cold pipes, takes time to flow. The bag doesn't sink as the bucket fills. It bobs. Finally he gets a rock, pushes the bag to the bottom, and sets the rock on top. He shudders.

"Are you okay?" she asks.

"I'm cold," he says.

He says he wants her at the airport to say goodbye. His mother drives. They sit together in the back. They hold hands. She does not tell him that she loves him, but she gives him a blue rabbit's foot on a keychain. "Good luck," and they kiss very awkwardly, because his mother is watching.

He sends her letters regularly. They're short, written on quarter sheets of off-blue paper, gaps between the words, big spaces between each line. It's not so bad here, is their theme. He sends her a pressed flower once.

He is home at Christmas. Snow falls, slow and heavy. They're driving around. On the dash are a Santa Hat and a box of condoms—presents from his father.

Earlier, he wanted to know, "Did you call your mother?" and now he is not speaking to her, unhappy with her answer.

She and her father have been fighting. A Friday in October he got careless near the end of his shift, left his hand down too long and had it mauled, his arm pulled half-off. Out on worker's-comp, her father is home all the time. So far as she can tell, he spends his days shirtless, stoking the fire and wandering from room to room, massaging the healing pink mess of his shoulder and drinking White Russians in consecutive gulps, like straight milk. Every time she comes through the door he's waiting for her, hell to pay.

She sent letters about it: her father's accident, her father's surgery, her father's uninterruptible anger after the hospital sends him, still hurting, home to her.

He was away for some sort of training when the accident first happened, without phone or mail for weeks. She felt badly at the time, knowing he would come back from wherever he was to a pile of her miserable news. He tried to call, but missed her, left a short message in a serious tone. "This is it for my phone time," he said. "I'll write you a letter."

He wrote that he was worried. He wanted her out of the house. She thought he meant she might somehow go to live with him. When he was first gone there had been one letter, longer than all the others, that gave her a panicky belly ache—*I'll buy you a washer and matching dryer and a smart little dog for company when I'm gone*—before it became her favorite.

She continues to keep the letter in her pillowcase—*I'll buy you a washer and matching dryer and a smart little dog for company when I'm gone*—though what he meant, when they finally coordinated a phone call, was that she should try to live with her mother.

"I saw her," she said, "but it doesn't matter."

"What's that mean?"

"It doesn't matter."

One night her father shoved her, and she fell back into the china hutch, putting an elbow through the glass. She didn't write him about that, or how she rode her bike into town, to the hospital where her mother works in billing and where her mother's new husband is a doctor in the emergency room.

Stitching her arm, the doctor, her stepfather, ignored her, speaking quick and angry to her mother, who stood hands-on-hips at the foot of the bed. "Lay with dogs," he said, "wake up with fleas. I can't have this. This is my work. Your kid shows up bashed up? What's next? People talk. People talk."

When the doctor left them her mother took her by the shoulders. "All better," she said brightly then leaned in close. "No tears. Don't embarrass me."

They saw one another again a few weeks later. Her mother asked her to meet at a restaurant. The doctor does not like children, and she has never been invited to the house where he and her mother live. As the host led them to a table, her mother took her hand. "Life," she said, "is ninety percent attitude. Don't let me hear anything but sunshine from you."

There is a fresh, knotty pink scar on her arm, but she hasn't taken her shirt off for him yet, and now they are driving around, not talking—he's mad—and she probably won't.

She thinks of the time when he cut his arm so badly it took seventeen stitches to close it, how she was the only one he would let hold his hand while they waited for the school nurse to come. It happened out on the playing field, where the shop class was building a temporary stage for a pep rally. People were crowding around him—prettier girls than her, uniformed cheerleaders she knew he'd slept with at parties before they started dating. Above their tall socks, the cheerleaders' knees were waxy white with cold, their eyes wet from the wind. They were pressing toward him cooing, but he said, "No," to all of them. "No," his bloody arm wrapped in a teacher's button-up, the other reaching out to her.

There are police lights behind them, strobing blue and white, but no siren. "Jesus fucked," he says and he pulls the car over. Rolling the window down, he tilts his face up, narrows his eyes, "What did I do?"

The officer bends. "No headlights," he says, breathing steam. Then, moving a gloved hand in the air, "It's night. It's snowing. Where're you comin' from, son?"

He answers, "Kosovo." When the officer asks for his license and registration, he asks, "Why?"

"Please," she whispers, touching the ticklish inside of his elbow, and watches his shoulders move, feels his anger rounding back on her.

Hidden behind the tights and socks and bras and underwear in her top dresser-drawer there are a year's worth of letters with *I love you* written in the margins.

The officer hands him back his ID, then across his body, tells her, "Step out."

She does. The officer takes her by the arm, looking her over. Her description is radio-ed in. Christmastime—the season of runaways. She looks young, and her boyfriend, the officer says, looks old. She has no ID. But the officer is checking for two missing girls, one a blonde, the other a natural redhead with hair dyed green and purple. She listens to their descriptions crackling back. Snow melts in her eyelashes, traces tiny trails of warmth over her chilled cheeks.

She is brown-haired with a red velvet ribbon for a headband. Christmastime, and he is home, is what she thought when she tied the bow.

The officer says, "Tell your boyfriend to turn his headlights on. Be careful," and his cruiser slides away into the snow spangled dark.

The passenger side door is locked. He's playing that trick—she grabs the handle, he pulls forward—stops—pulls forward again. When she starts crying he unlocks the door and lets her get into the car. He says, "Look, sorry. Christ. Stop."

Taking the ribbon from her hair, he twists it between his fingers. When he holds his hand out, she ties the ends into a bow at his wrist.

He says, "I'm gonna drop you off."

Her history class is interrupted by the intercom. The teacher listens then nods to her; she is wanted in the main office. She expects to be busted for skipping study hall, but rather than give her a detention slip the receptionist waves her past. "Go on through to the principal, honey."

Outside his office, the principal is waiting. He guides her through the door with a hand on her back. "You're not in trouble," he says. "Sit."

She sits. Her feet don't touch the floor. She crosses her ankles. She folds her hands.

The principal says, "I have some news to tell you." He clears his throat. "Your boyfriend—"

He's disappeared. Run off. That morning, he was slow moving. When his bunkmate said, "You'd better haul ass, man," he answered he was coming, lay off. It's later in the day that someone realizes he's not where he's supposed to be. Someone is sent to find him. They can't. He is searched for, but he is gone.

Midway through his recounting, the principal's sympathy breaks. He sweats out the word, "AWOL," as if it's his own son they're discussing. On the desktop, his curled fists tighten, release, and squeeze, a strained pulse that makes her think of two giant snails forced from the protection of their shells. She cannot meet the principal's eye, instead watching the narrow bones move under the skin of the backs of his hands. When he shifts all his weight forward and says accusingly, "Now, missy, you must know—" she reflexively flinches. He falters then softens. He clears his throat. "This is a real pickle, isn't it?"

She leaves the principal's office with a short list of numbers: an army counselor, a sergeant, his mother's new home phone. The paper is damp with sweat, the lines of ink feathering. In the hall, the principal asks her to make a promise. "You have him use those." She draws a sincere X across her heart.

The first day of waiting she is breathless, sleepless, brainless. Hours pass one second at a time. The next day is the same: near infinite. She begins to feel like air. Then the third day arrives without him, or any word of him—nothing from him, nothing about him.

Nothing.

She closes her eyes, opens them, and tries to see the world differently.

Alone in the kitchen, she fixes herself a bowl of cereal. A tremor in her hand clatters the spoon against her teeth. Milk spills down her chin and following the line of her throat, rides the rise of her breasts to dampen her bra.

Six weeks later—she goes for milkshakes with a boy from her English Class. He pays. They sit at a table near the window where the radiator runs along the wall. Outside, a heavy drizzle makes everything soft-edged and gray. She needs new boots. Her feet are wet and cold. She fogs the glass with her breath then uses the heel of her hand to clear a circle. A blurred man and woman run past, pushing a baby buggy zipped in translucent plastic.

The boy taps his long sundae spoon against the tiled tabletop. He asks her, "So what about that other guy?"

She knows what she should say—*it doesn't matter now*—but that's a lie she hasn't yet taught herself to tell.

Vickie

On the side of the highway you take to get anywhere here, there's a billboard for a chain of steakhouses with this gem of a slogan: *There's no such thing as a chicken knife.* Ending with a period, rather than an exclamation point, because there isn't anything to get excited over. It's a fact: there *is* no such thing as a chicken knife.

The billboard sits above a hundred or so small white crosses angled in rows to face the lanes. A plywood sign with red lettering that dripped before it dried is planted alongside them: *Choose Life.*

It took me longer than it should have to make the correct connection. Yes, I did read the sign as a message of affirmation, but not at all as intended. It took my breath away, passing by the first time. I was that eager to interpret it as fate, a nod of approval from the universe, agreeing I'd done the right thing in pulling up stakes, coming here to start anew.

The flat fields of mud streaked by, lifeless, and I thought: *I have chosen life.*

The second time, I was certain the field must have been the scene of a crash. I was coming back then from the first day of work in a warehouse with walls like a kindergarten classroom: all nooks for little children's little things, but all big enough for me to stand in on tiptoes, hands stretched above my head. The giant cubbies held pallets of flat screen TVs, and bestselling paperback books, charcoal detoxifying teas, gift baskets with caviar, and coloring sets with 152 crayons.

Not new to this kind of work, I was allowed, in my first hour, to operate the hydraulic scaffolding and retrieve the luxury goods kept up high. "We're impressed," said the man who gave me access, "with your skills," and how, at that—*my skills*—could my heart not hang its head? All day, I fetched then sent expensive things down a conveyor belt for unseen men and women to wrap and box and label and send away.

Choose Life, I thought—the words dull under the orange smear of the early evening sky—encouraged drivers to operate their vehicles with greater care. I imagined a clichéd sort of super-tragedy: a caravan of buses full of school children, hurtling down the highway toward an amusement park, their screams of joy becoming screams of terror as metal compressed around them.

For my initial lack of understanding, here is the only excuse I can offer: though living in the South, I am not native to it. The lure—a lower cost of living, the freedom of being unknown, swaying palms and sandy beaches—always hides a hook. The first time that a kind young Baptist began to proselytize—"Do you ever think about how we're all children in the family of man?"—I thought he was insane, and tried to fend him off with a dollar. Then I laid up through the night, asking myself, *What proof is there, what proof, that we're all children in the family of man?*

Now, I've watched the phlox bloom, the mud transformed to the surface of a shallow, purple sea. Mothers whip their mini-vans into the gravel and glass at the roadside, take a step, and plop plump babies down in the flowers for photos, the air currents from the passing eighteen-wheelers sometimes ripping their little white hats from their little curly heads, spinning them out into traffic.

Once, on a rural highway tracing the gray edge of the Atlantic, I saw a little girl, practically a baby, alone and without a coat in an over-grown lawn of winter-yellow grass. Set far behind her was a falling-down farm house with a roof patterned like houndstooth, so many of its slate shingles were missing. Snow was falling like powdered sugar: soft, soft—a dusting.

The girl ran toward the car holding out fists full of dried Queen Anne's Lace, all the tiny white stars of petals passed, but I knew the toothy brown crown of it dead. A sound was rolling out of me, involuntary and raw, and I was depressing the brake, certain it would do no good.

Luck—that I didn't hit her. Before I didn't, I knew I would, and I was screaming because I'd killed a child and though it happened it yet, it would. I knew it would. In less than a second, it would.

But the girl stopped with one foot on the tar, the other in the strip of frost-laced sand at the shoulder, round-eyed, the brittle bones of flowers falling from her fright loosened hands. The sound I had made was still ringing all around.

I had to think to breathe. Imagine the steady press of water. Air precious. Hold. Release.

Cutting the engine, I rolled the window down, "Little girl?"

A season gone—the sign's red lettering has flaked away, and though the board is emptied of words, I can read them there still. And still I wonder, having sorted out one connection—those crosses, that plywood sign—why is it that when I pass the field at a rate of speed so slowed it could be called meditative, rather than fill my time with counting and tallying imaginary lives, I cannot help but think of Vickie Flower?

From kindergarten until junior high, we were in the same class: Vickie and Vickie. We shared a name. My mother appreciated her for someone who lived a life of greater extremes. While some days, I did not have the dollar to pay for the hot lunch the cafeteria served and had to "borrow" a meal, my name recorded in a little book by the teacher's aide, a note sent home at the end of the week, Vickie Flower was given her lunches for free. If we were poor, the Flowers were as poor as dirt. My father, who had a reputation of his own, called them that, "Dirt," when he heard the family's name, and my mother nodded slow and serious. "That's right." There is comfort, she sought to teach, in comparison and the careful work of categorizing: *A place for everything and everything in its place.*

In the apartment complex where I live now in the South, the pool doesn't ever officially close. For aesthetics it's kept-up year round, but

I'm the only one who uses it in winter. The fountain at its center regurgitates water unadmired while I swim laps. When I'm there, natives, passing, eye the water with distinct distaste. "Cold enough for ya?" is the question frequently posed.

As a child back North, I broke a glaze of ice with each forward stroke of my hands. Behind the yellow house we rented, a snarl of sea heather led down to brown green water. Six rivers met there, mixing with the ocean. At low tide a thin shimmer of water, ankle deep, with the coarse shine of sugar, spread for miles. At high tide dark water lapped at the heather and I could part its purple columns and fall forward, knowing I would be caught in its wet clasp. Winter here settles in the sixties. A mild breeze shuffles the enormous fronds, verdant until the heat of summer begins to fray them.

I do a log roll, and come up dripping.

Watching, the natives shiver.

"It's not so bad," I say.

Sometimes they stay and make light, if slightly accusatory conversation through the fence. There is a woman who slows to make the observation, "You've got your own private pool there," each time she passes, using a tone that lets me know she thinks it is unfair. That she could swim but chooses not to doesn't matter. In her mind it is a luxury she cannot afford and one I flaunt.

Who, I see this woman think, *does she think she is?*

Vickie stole my crayons and my pencils. In winter, she stole my ChapStick and my ninety-nine cent stretch gloves. She stole the paper snowflakes I made to hang in the window, adding, after my name, the letter F.

Any little thing she could fit into her pockets, she stole, and as we grew larger, larger things too. One day, she took my winter coat. As we filed out onto the playground, she lifted it from my hook on the wall. Above it was strip of tape, labeled *Vickie*. I watched her struggling into it, the back too narrow, the shoulders tight.

I didn't want to tell.

Outside, I huddled in a stand of trees, trying to stay out of the wind and go unnoticed by the playground aides. Vickie came and stood in

front of me. She worked the brass zipper up and down—*z i n g z i n g.*
"You're so poor," she heckled. "You're so poor you don't even have a coat."

When I came home without it, my mother, furious, called the school, though I begged her not to. "It has fur," she snapped, dialing. "Real fur."

I like the shadows that things floating on the water make. What I thought was a large insect wing, is a leaf, veins and chambers exposed. Waves of water make waves of shadow on the turquoise concrete. I like how my hair looks underwater, like a rarely seen living thing found only in the deepest, coldest, darkness which no human can penetrate and survive, and I like how my voice sounds when it's submerged, like a happy drunk, looping and full of heavy silver bubbles, and I like the way my heart beats in my ears, how it is a hard-textured sound, steady and slow, like hopscotch—the flat impact and report of a hollow plastic boot heel against the macadam in the schoolyard.

Vickie was so unlikable she was difficult even to pity. She stole, she stole, she stole, and she lied, and she swore, and she bullied.

Once, she and I were the only ones who didn't bring the money for a field trip. Left behind, we sat side by side at the back of our classroom. The lights were off. Outside the bright morning sun had broken, hatching a dull, chilly afternoon. At the front of the room, a library assistant sat at our teacher's desk, a cart of books beside her. She was flipping through them, an eraser in her hand. Every so often she would sigh, rub violently at a page, then tilt her face down and blow it clean of shredded pink rubber.

"Hey," Vickie whispered. We'd been given strips cut from magazines and sheets of slitted construction paper to weave them through. "I heard your mother got a job—" I looked over "—sucking dicks." If I did not understand the insult exactly, I still knew it was ugly. I began to cry. Vickie rocked in her seat, giggling, a sweet, carefree sound.

When the woman from the leasing office gave me a tour of the complex, she focused on the amenities: the pool, the updated laundry room, the ceiling fans that would keep the cost of air conditioning down, the spacious clubhouse available to rent for special occasions. A pink helium balloon drifted along the ceiling. "We just had," she said, "a quinceanera." She scraped a wadded pink napkin into the trash. "You better believe I got *that* deposit in cash."

Back in the office, I asked what I thought were responsible questions: Extra fees?

Maintenance?

Crime?

The woman looked at me levelly, "I can't go into that. We don't release that information." She folded her hands in front of her. "For a budget, this is a nice place. You can practically smell the Gulf." Then she leaned forward, "But the north side of the complex is *especially* nice."

On the wall, was a plan of the complex. Using her fingernail, the woman slowly drew an X over a long building at the back. "You might request," she said, "something at the front?" Her features squeezed, her eyelids fluttering. It took me a moment to understand she was trying to wink.

My mother cleaned summer cottages in the off-season, sweeping the dark seeds that were mouse droppings off the countertops and duvets, dusting, popping in to set a faucet dripping against a hard freeze, a light switched on one night and off the next to dissuade local teenagers from gently breaking-in and drinking the liquor cabinet dry before sex on the plaid sofas. It was a job where she could bring me along, keeping me clear of my father and his unpredictable moods, and had the added bonus odd hours, allowing her to serve as a constant volunteer at my school.

She came to the classroom dressed in pearls, in cardigans, in little leather-heeled shoes. At the consignment shop in town, she was a menace. The glamorized woman at the register always said, "Look who's found the best things," though her lips were thinned as she unhooked the tiny brass safety pins and filed away the price tags. My mother's clothes, and that she drove a sports car—an MG Midget that had been her mother's—gave, initially, a deceptive impression. Everything of obvious value was leftover from a previous life I had not known, the selective pickings of someone else's half-used luxuries.

When we shopped for groceries, my mother kept a running tabulation of how much had been spent, and before entering the line for the register, deliberated, having to choose what must go back to the shelves. She would say, "I think that's good. I think we're fine now," but her math was bad, or dreamy.

Until I was much older, I thought it was a common thing, regular practice, for a woman to reject a purchase after it was rung-up. "Oh," my mother would say, dismissive, annoyed, "I don't want that." She behaved as if the items that we could not afford had ended up in her cart through some sort of hijinks; a joke had been pulled on her and she was not amused. By the time the receipt was printed, the cashier had an unsteady pyramid of returns stacked beside her.

On occasion, we found ourselves behind Vickie's mother, Mrs. Flower, and watched her buying her groceries with food stamps color-coded like Monopoly money. They didn't seem to come in denominations larger than ten, so it was always a ruffling sheaf that Mrs. Flower handed over. Time was tied up in the exchange. There were only two checkout lanes, and the cashier was either a very young woman, or a very old woman, and blushing with embarrassment, or inflicted with palsy, she would fumble the fistful of pink and green paper and have to count it again.

Mrs. Flower stabbed at the air, an unlit cigarette between two knuckles. She spoke just audibly, and not to anyone in particular. "Where'd they get *you*. What're *you* good for." Like Vickie, she had small, rounded teeth evenly spaced in her mouth, and light brown eyes, down-turned at their outer edges. Like her daughter, she was beautiful.

Watching Mrs. Flower, my mother's body grew tighter and tighter. When she was angry, she shrank like cooking meat. I watched her pull in on herself watching the Flower's food moving slowly along the conveyer belt: long foam trays of chicken nuggets, gallon jugs of bright green juice, soda, popsicles, potato chips, flat boxes of frozen manicotti, powdered donuts. Half of it, things I had agitated for, knowing better.

At school I sometimes watched Vickie during snack-time, tearing packages with her teeth, assembling mini pizzas or nachos from multichambered plastic containers. For me, my mother used the heels from the loaf of bread. My father would not eat the ends, but *waste not want not*. She made a sandwich with crust-sides facing-in, stuck together with peanut butter. I brought home the bag that had held it, and she turned it inside out, rinsed it, and clothespinned it to the skinny sill above the sink to dry.

Sometimes, I go out walking at night. I lap the complex buildings until I start to sweat, then go back to my apartment to take a bath and sit up until I'm tired. People don't think of someone out in the dark, moving slowly—how with a light on, their blinds don't even need to be opened, only angled the slightest bit, for someone outside to see in.

What I see, mostly, are empty rooms, like my rooms are empty when I'm not inside them. I see that there is only one apartment, duplicated again and again, so that everyone's rooms are my rooms—the same size, the same shape—yet, some are beautiful. There is one apartment where the walls in the kitchen have been painted shocking red, and all the furniture is shiny-black and matching. I cannot, or rather, I can *only*, imagine opening the door and having those rooms be "home."

But, if the red kitchen is beyond my grasp, then what I have is out of reach for someone else. There are apartments worse than mine: rabbit-holed plaster, and gritty carpets. Through broken blinds, I see a recliner whose cushions are collapsed in the shape of a man, the upholstery tarry where hands settle, the antimacassar centered on its back, an orange halo of grease. In a different living room, on a bare mattress on the floor, a woman sleeps with the lights on, a child's cartoon print comforter wrapped around her hips.

On the roadside that day, I cut the engine and left the car. "Little girl?" She came to me with her arms raised in a child's universal gesture: *Pick me up.* No one had burst from the house at the shriek of the brakes. There was no distant voice, strained, calling for a child slipped out of sight. The little girl was alone, and shivering, and asking with her empty hands to be taken into mine.

I didn't force her into the car. When I lifted her, she put her arms around my neck. I only meant to make sure she wasn't hurt, and then I was holding her and thought I if I took her, I could prevent the hurts I knew would come.

I have a bed, a mop, and a broom. I sweep and it gets smaller, gathering its own bristles, but it's mine. I have a good table. I have a good chair. I have a television too, taken from a high shelf in the warehouse. Past the round black eyes of the cameras, the one positioned over the time clock, the one positioned over the door, I carried it out. Newness preserved, still in its box, sealed with copper staples and strips of tape, I keep it tipped against the living room wall.

If confronted I'll ask to return it. My apology will be sincere. I'll tell the truth: "I made a mistake."

Tacked to the wall above the television in its box, is a print of a Renaissance drawing. The truth is, I took that too, from an open display in a library. It was pinned to a felt board, not under glass. Left out like that, it seemed it could be easily replaced. It is a woman with a belly made of snakes. They're eating their way out of her. Across the bottom is a banner. In the banner is the word: *Envy.* The light, reflecting off the pool water, moves across the wall in sinuous ripples. At the right time of day, when the position of the sun is just so, the snakes, ink on paper, come to writhing life.

Vickie became a smarter thief. The day after my mother called about the coat she'd stolen, I watched her arrive to school wearing it. She'd made crude alterations, hacking away the fur trim. A frizzle of soft cured skin and loose thread dangled just above her pretty wrists. Across her shoulders, it pulled tight. On the playground, waiting for first bell, she stood with her arms at her sides, unable to lift them, but almost stylish, and presumably warm.

A man from the leasing office is showing apartments. Two people trail behind him. When the path brings the trio close enough for me to hear their individual voices, it becomes clear that the pair receiving the tour are an undergraduate and her nervous father.

"We'll miss her, but she thinks it's time." As he's speaking, the father tries to put an arm around the daughter, and she sidesteps out of reach. "She's ready." He forces a laugh, gesturing to the empty space beside him.

The man from the office is oblivious. "I know," he answers, "believe me, I know how hard it is to watch them go."

The father asks, "How old are yours?"

"I—" the man pauses. He plucks at his shirt then raises his hand to shield his eyes, looking toward the sun. "Might be a hot one," he says. "Might heat up today."

The father says, "She's our youngest."

The man admits, "I don't have my own."

In the pool, I have been indulging, doing kid tricks: hand stands and somersaults, sinking to sit on the bottom to drink imaginary tea. Fun and games has earned me water in my ears and distorted hearing—all words begin and end on a slight wobble. As a result, everyone sounds on the verge of tears.

The man from the office consults his clipboard. "What should I show you next?"

Recently, the complex has shifted hands and "improvements" have been made. The walkways power washed, and the buildings, formerly a smoky blue, repainted in complementary pastels, the ripped window screens replaced, and as a final touch, a wide spaced row of young palms planted between the parking lot and street. The new owners are going for a beach-y feel, though we are just far enough from the ocean to be landlocked. In keeping, all the staff now wear a uniform: a white polo shirt and khaki shorts. Everyone must be responsible for providing their own, because no one's short-and-shirt-set is the same. When I go to the office to pay my rent and see employees side-by-side, the effect is that of schoolgirls who have decided to celebrate their friendship by "being twins," trying to accomplish interchangeability through passing similarity.

The trio—the man from the office, the daughter, and the father—are walking the fence line outside the pool, working their way to the gate. On the far side of the palms, a car propels around the turn in a throb of music and is gone. Charged with bass vibration, the concrete lip of the pool hums under my hand. The father stops the small group's progress to ask about the neighborhood.

The man from the office points out the grilling area and the Emergency Phone Box that dials 9-1-1 if the handset is lifted from the cradle. "We care about our residents," he says.

The father asks again about the neighborhood, and the daughter sighs, crossing her arms.

"Well, that's a good question." The man from the office pauses, thinking. Finally, he says, "It's developing."

"Developing?" The father is apologetic. "I don't know what that means."

The daughter, a few steps ahead now, stops and scuffs at the concrete. Her hair is in a ponytail, and I bob watching her slowly twist the end around and around her finger. She says, "Maybe it means it's *developing*."

The father turns on her so fast his clothing makes a lash of color in the air. "I'm sorry," he says. "I'm so sorry." His shoulders are squaring, pulling him taller. "I'm sorry," and now his voice is rising, becoming shrill. "I'm sorry." He takes a step toward her, and the girl ducks her head, bringing up her hands to hide her face. The father takes another step. "I'm sorry that I like to know where I'm putting my money."

I like the calmness of water. I like the security of it—how it holds a body unbothered. I like to let myself sink, knowing I will float. Water is a balm, but I am like a hot pan doused. I could turn water into steam.

The man from the office angles past the daughter and opens the gate onto the patio. In the shallow water, I have sunk down. I am floating like a crocodile, eyes just above the surface.

Bending to dip his fingertips, the man from the office does not initially see me. When he does, he's startled. Lamely, he says, "And here's our training Olympian."

Moving on they look at the plastic lounge chairs and glass topped tables, the fountain and the decorative waterfall tumbling a chlorinated froth.

I hear the daughter ask, "Can you smoke out here?"

The man from the office, pitched so the father will not hear, answers, "Depends what you're smoking."

As they are leaving, the father slows and looks again at everything around him. I see the instant he understands the freshness of the paint, the rawness of the open earth around the juvenile palms, the heaviness, not only of chlorine, but of bleach in the air. I see him seeing through the surface. Now, he is offended by the waste of his time.

For a moment, I stare at his retreating back and think, with disgust, *people.*

But who I am to judge human ugliness?

Beside me in the car the little girl was not afraid. She sat small in the seat, babbling in child-speak. Her knees were like teacups overturned. My palm covered the round of bone, warming her cold skin.

Autumn was slipping in winter. Dusk made a sudden descent. The sky was arranged like a parfait, gauzy blue, then slate streaked orange, and new snow was falling, a pretty dusting of flakes against the fresh dark. The tops of the pines became blackish-silver like a tangle of hooks. How long had we been driving?

Not long.

Not long, when I turned back.

At school, some of the mothers humored mine, and others did not. There were women who were amused by her—how she leaned close, how she giggled, how she gossiped, hiding her mouth behind her hands—and there were women who could see the labor behind her presentation and did not care for it.

There was one girl, Andrea Ely, whose white haired father was a judge. When her mother was asked what her husband did, she said breezily, "Oh, something with the law…" Judge Ely. "Oh, something with the law…"

My father was not a carpenter, but he built things from wood. He considered himself an artist, and had quit school his sophomore year. To make ends meet, he sold what he said were "detox pills" to high school boys. They were goldenseal capsules, repackaged in wax paper bags designed for penny candies. With them, my father prescribed drinking two full gallons of water a day, which was enough to flush a system for a basic urine test. The stairs of our back porch were often un-navigable for the bodies of teenage boys sprawling them.

When my mother was young, my father's ne'er-do-wellism and self-importance must have appealed to her. He would have cut a bad-boy figure. But, when it was the three of us together, he made her anxious, apologetic, sometimes frantic. At the table, my father would bring his fist down, "Look at me." And then, "Don't you *dare* look at me like that."

One night he called us out to the shed where he worked. His back was to us, but as we came through the door, he turned. Over the lower half his face, worn like a bandit's mask, were a pair of my mother's underwear. He said, "Something's fishy here," and laughed. My mother spun away, but my father grabbed her arm. With her free hand she pushed me toward the door.

"Go," she said.

"Come here," he said.

On his workbench, quartered and beheaded, was a toy of mine, a fake Barbie—the hollow kind with legs that had rough seams and tinsel hair.

He pulled the underwear down around his neck. He spread his arms. "Whaddaya think?"

My mother shook her head.

"What do you think?" he asked again, and every word quick and clear and sharp. "What do you think? What do you think?"

My mother was cautious. "What should I think?"

"What *should* you think?"

She hesitated.

From a drawer in the workbench, he pulled out a fat book, flipping pages. He showed us a photograph—a tea towel stiff with dried blood, punctured with nails and glass. "That's Picasso!"

My mother moved me behind her. I put my face against her back. She asked him, "What should I say?"

"What *should* you say?"

She started to cry. I could feel it, her back jumping against my cheek. "Just tell me what to say."

My father was gone the next morning, but his things stayed. Erratically, he reappeared and my mother would send me to bed, asking him softly to tuck me in, which sometimes, he did. Some mornings, I would find him standing in the kitchen, shirtless, smoking over the sink, my mother pressed to his back, her hands splayed across his stomach. She was whispering, "A twenty, if you have it. For lunch money and new used boots. Just a twenty," pressing kisses to his shoulders and neck. She saw me, and she shook her head, and I knew to go back to my room.

My father continued to attend select functions and certain holiday celebrations, the jittering man who would hug us both briefly in the parking lot outside the school's auditorium, asking, "Are we done now?"

My mother always thanked him. Sometimes, as my father pulled back, she would not let go, arms around his waist, head laid on his shoulder, and I could see that though she was scared of him, she was scared to be without him. He would reach back and unlink her hands and she would delicately catch his cuff between two fingers, asking, "Do you want to come home with us? Do you have anything for us?"

After he left, my mother would say, "Your father loves you very much."

I had never seen Mr. Flower. I had never heard mention of Vickie having a father. Once, she saw mine. In the same class, our names back to back, her parent-teacher conference followed mine. An area of the library had been turned into a waiting room. A banner reading: *Readers Become Leaders*, was tacked above a table with a coffee urn and paper cups and a cylinder of powdered creamer. Coffee stirrers and bookmarks were arranged in fans. Elsewhere, there were playgroups and art projects underway, but older children could be left there alone in the library waiting area while parents went to meetings.

When my teacher came to collect my parents, my father refused to go. My mother plucked at his sleeve. "Please. Please."

He shrugged her off with a roll of his shoulder. "You go."

She did, and he stayed with me, arms crossed, overwhelming a child-sized plastic chair, staring at the floor. I made him a cup of coffee. I held it out in front of him until he looked up and said, "You think I want that? Are you stupid? What's wrong with you?"

I dropped the cup. A hot puddle spread around my feet. My father pushed me, not roughly, just back and out of the spill. There were no napkins. He laid down a handful of bookmarks. Immediately, they were dark. I brought him more. "Get away," he said. "You aren't helping. Get away from me."

I turned, and there was Vickie sitting quietly on the floor, Mrs. Flower in a chair behind her, watching blankly. I could feel the tears starting in my throat. I wanted a corner behind the bookshelves where my father would not see me. More than that, I wanted for Vickie not to have seen. As I passed her, she rocked up into a squat, "You gonna cry?" She followed me, apelike, hunched and on folded knuckles.

I didn't want to leave the little girl as I'd found her, but I did. Rounding the curve of the road, I had expectations of rolling blue police lights and angry silhouettes. But the only change was a room lit inside the house. The little girl, like a monkey with a nut, was studying my hand on her knee. A tiny fingertip stroked across the wrinkled ridges of each knuckle. "Home again," I said to her, and was realizing this could no longer be my home, that I had a done a thing deserving of exile and the forfeiture of anything I had made for myself, and I unbuckled the little girl's safety belt and I leaned across her little body to open the door. She was still intent on the study of my hand. I pulled away, pushing gently, then more firmly. Night was slipping down, and I left her just as I'd found her—cold, and coatless, alone.

Two wrongs, I was told in childhood, do not make a right.

Today it was unseasonably warm and there were women at the pool. At a table, under the shade of an umbrella, they were drinking strawberry wine coolers and laughing. The babies that had come from them were the small children running unattended along the water's edge. I wanted to leave, but did not want to be driven off, and could not help but worry about the children. The women, both steadily getting drunk, traded wine coolers for sweating, jumbo plastic cups. An older child, an undeveloped girl, maybe ten, in a turquoise ruffled bikini sized for an adult, was an ad-hoc lifeguard in moments of extreme peril. When the youngest child, a toddler, dressed in only a diaper, began crawling down the steps into the water, she called sharply, but was ignored. We watched—all of us—as the baby tumbled face first into the pool. The girl was quick to jump in after it, quick to fish it out. The force of her entrance into the water displaced her bikini top. She came up with the wailing toddler, and one flat breast exposed.

A man came to the fence, eager. "Is everything okay?"

"I'm not with them."

Under the umbrella, laughter folded the women in on themselves. One wolf whistled. The other hooted, "Look at you! Look at you!" The girl set the baby, still screaming, on the patio, and covered herself. It toddled from her, toward the women, arms up, howling for comfort. Leaning forward, one grabbed the baby by the shoulder, holding its wet body back. It shrieked. The woman pushed it away then raised her leg, putting a foot against its chest, demanding, "Leave me alone."

When my mother volunteered, she loved to reprimand Vickie: "No, Vickie. Vickie, wait your turn. Vickie Flower, where are your manners?" Then when Vickie had been made to file through the line, and was up to receive her cup of punch, or select what pipe cleaners she would use, or be fitted for the paper headdress she would wear in the holiday recital, some other infraction became apparent. "Vickie, your hands are filthy." I flinched when I heard it—my name, like that, from my mother's mouth.

Two things more alike than not—who could help but to compare them? To make sense of the world and all its parts we divide and categorize using the simplest system possible: good and bad. Given two things, we identify each as the other's opposites. Whether they are or not, does not truly matter.

Still, beside Vickie, I should have shined. I believe that was my mother's hope. Instead, I disappeared.

Someone said our name. I looked up. I said, "Yes?" I said, "Ma'am?" I was that sort of child. But no one was speaking to me. We sat in alphabetized rows, Vickie always a foot away. "No one's talking to *you*," she said.

Eventually, I stopped answering, so rarely did anyone mean me.

I like to be at the pool alone. When I come up from the water, it has nothing in common with Venus rising from her shell, the waves unfurling behind her. Alone, that doesn't matter. Alone, there is nothing to prove or to improve. There is no one there to notice. With no one for comparison, I am anyone I like. I am myself, alone, and the only needs that I need be concerned with are my own.

Andrea Ely, who I invited to my birthday party, who said she could not come, because I lived in an apartment, spent a night at Vickie's. Curious about how the Flowers lived, she invited herself to a sleepover. In her recounting of the night, Andrea focused on her own deviousness, how with her mother away, she duped her clueless father—who had no grasp of rules and procedures, who did not know that mothers speak to mothers over the phone before anything is arranged, and walk their child to the door to peek inside before leaving them—into letting her out in the driveway, coming to collect her the next morning. Information about the actual sleepover came from Andrea's answers to questions asked by other girls in our class. I sat at the edge of their circle, not invited in, but ignored and so allowed to listen.

Andrea described a general dampness in the house, an unpleasant smell, the shock of turning a corner and finding a person, *a teenager*, crouched there, smoking in a dark hallway. Down in the basement, Vickie had a makeshift room. It was cold. Instead of a door, a shower curtain with fish on it had been nailed to the frame. They were there, Andrea singing along with the portable radio, when Mr. Flower—Vickie called the man Dad—came downstairs and slapped Vickie so hard her head bounced off the wall.

Because her company was too loud.

Andrea, from a different world entirely, could not, even having seen it, understand the details so well as I—everything in that house was so foreign to her. Andrea didn't even know to be scared.

Though I swim laps, the pool here is really a sunbathers' pool. At its deepest, it's six feet. There is the fountain at the center, a little foaming waterfall, and one whole side is a smooth, faux stone gradation meant for lounge chairs, so that people can tan while dangling their toes in the water. When girls are doing this, there are men who do chin-ups hanging from the lip of the little waterfall. They grunt and strain, though their activities are effortless. They are performing. I've watched this sort of posing all my life—people assuming an attitude for the benefit of a select audience.

"Vickie," our teacher said, "you're not in any trouble. But I want you to tell the truth." She spoke in a kind voice, louder than was necessary.

At the back of the room, my mother and Mrs. Ely were demonstrating how a brown paper bag might be transformed into an exciting "safari vest." We were studying the Amazon, and too old for dress up and pretend besides, which my mother knew, but Mrs. Ely had saved and brought in all her grocery bags. "Isn't this fun," my mother insisted, fitting brown paper over the shoulders of a sulking classmate, but watching me.

Our teacher said, "Vickie, I know you want to tell the truth." She was holding a coat. It was black wool with a hood trimmed in stiff fake fur, and a placket with six shiny, metal buttons, similar to the coat I'd had the year before—the coat Vickie had stolen, that my mother had cried for, because she could not replace it.

"Vickie," our teacher asked, "is this yours?" She prompted, "Vickie?" At the back of the room, my mother nodded.

"Vickie?" the teacher asked again. Neither of us spoke. The teacher held the coat out. My mother smiled, nodded. I took it. It was Vickie's, but I wore it home.

When the sunlight makes the humid air a milky haze—sunburn weather, the natives call it—the pool is all but abandoned. I have it to myself. Turning on my back, I let the water hold me. I close my eyes, and feel the heat, a simple pleasure. And for a moment, there is *only* pleasure, and then the little girl is with me. I see her in the dark of my closed eyes. I see how I left her, cold and coatless, alone.

My mother met me at the apartment door. She held herself strangely, her hands clasped together at her waist. She said, "You've gotten your coat back."

"It doesn't fit."

She ushered me inside. "You'll grow into it. It's classic."

I understood then that she must have said something to the teacher, that she had lied, that she had said the coat was mine, and she meant for us to pretend that, in my taking it, a wrong had been righted.

My mother stooped down to roll the sleeves, too long for my arms. She smoothed the fur around the hood. "You," she said, "are the most beautiful girl I've ever seen."

I have given myself a new rule. I leave the pool when other people come. I do not think I should allow myself to glut on pleasure. So I go. Because when I stay, now that the weather is warming, I see those two women with their small children, the toddler allowed to run around in only a diaper, and the older girl, put in charge of all the other kids. *Trash*, I think. I watch those loud women wheeling their cooler over the concrete, and I think, *I am not much, but I am better than you*—and I like that feeling more than I would like to.

I wore Vickie's coat to school. It was a low-skied day, clouds stacked like shale—the fierce kind of cold that births a weak storm. At recess, a fine, stinging snow began to fall. The playground aides stood at the door, clanging a bell, calling us in. Vickie stepped alongside me. She was wearing a man's sweatshirt. It covered her hands and hung past her knees. She leaned close to whisper, "You're a liar."

Because she was right, because she was telling the truth, and I was ashamed, I wanted badly to hurt her. I used the cruelest words I knew. "You're just trash."

She laughed and then she looked away. "I know."

Acknowledgments

Grateful acknowledgment is made to the editors of the publications in which these stories, some in alternate versions, first appeared: *Alaska Quarterly Review, Catapult, Cimarron Review, Colorado Review, Epoch, Georgia Review, Michigan Quarterly Review*, and *Shenandoah*.

My most heartfelt thanks to T.M. McNally, Alberto Rios, Tara Ison, Krista Ratcliffe, Diane Goettel, and Yvonne Garrett for their support.

Thank you to B, K, O, and N for your friendship, which I am grateful for every day.

Photo: Brad Irish

Jenny Irish is from Maine, but lives in Tempe, Arizona, where she is an Assistant Professor in the Creative Writing Program at Arizona State University. Her first collection is *Common Ancestor.*